RECIPES
for the
HEART

ANDI WHITEFIELD

ISBN 978-1-0980-3841-0 (paperback)
ISBN 978-1-0980-3842-7 (digital)

Christian Faith Publishing, Inc.
832 Park Avenue
Meadville, PA 16335
www.christianfaithpublishing.com

Printed in the United States of America

For my niece, Lindsey Carson,
God's mighty warrior.

CONTENTS

ACKNOWLEDGMENTS

Praise and honor to my heavenly Father for helping me write this book and showing me how to wait upon the Lord.

Special thanks to my mother, Anita Mckinley, and my mother-in-law, Linda Ballard, for sharing your delicious recipes.

Thank you to my cherished sisters in Christ, Yvonne, Audrey, Deborah, and Alexandra. Your love, friendship, and prayers are such a blessing.

Thanks to my friend Kathy Walker. I am grateful for your powerful prayers and words of encouragement.

Many thanks to my friend Kathy Herd. Your sincere life for Christ was an inspiration when writing this book.

Thank you to my sister in Christ Veronica Jefferson. Your continued prayer and words of truth are such a blessing.

Sincere thanks to my friend Evelyn Lang. Your loveliness gave me the idea for my character's name (Evelyn).

Thank you to my sister Amy English for being my proofreader.

Much love to my children, Drew and Taylor, for always helping me in my struggles with technology.

Love and gratitude to my husband, Quint, for believing in me.

CHAPTER 1

Looking to Jesus in Life's Storms

It was a humid summer morning. There was a continuous line of thunderstorms moving across the area. Me and Momma were on our way to the hospital, which was fifty miles away. My stepdad, Roy, had been in and out of the hospital for over a year. It was taking a toll on Momma. She had been suffering from dementia for quite a while, and it was upsetting to her when Roy was gone.

My sister, Daisy, and I had decided that they needed a caregiver to help them out when Roy returned home from the hospital. I had no idea how to find someone, how would I be able to locate someone trustworthy and kind. My mind was in a fog.

As I merged onto the interstate, the rain started pouring down. I gripped the steering wheel and began to pray, "Lord, please keep me and Momma safe."

My life had become a sudden violent rainstorm. I couldn't seem to see my way out of the sudden crisis. I felt as if things could spin out of control at any minute.

We crept along the highway with the other cars. Some of the vehicles didn't seem to be bothered by the deluge of water as they sped past. In the distance, I could see emergency lights flashing on the right side of the road. As we came closer, I moved over to the left lane. I could see a fire truck and an ambulance up ahead. All the sudden, I hit a low spot in the road, and my car began to hydroplane slightly before gripping the pavement again. I regained control as my heart pounded, and adrenaline surged through my body.

When we reached the accident, we could see that there was a vehicle upside down in the ditch. They were loading up the driver into the ambulance. The emergency crew were doing their best to quickly and safely transport the patient in the blinding wind and rain. Up ahead, I spotted an exit. I told Momma that I was going to pull off for a few minutes to let the storm pass. As I pulled off, I could see a church on the left side of the road. I drove into the parking lot and put the car in park. I loosened my grip from the steering wheel and tried to relax for a moment.

Momma sat next to me, rattling on and repeating the same stories. She asked me once again why Roy was in the hospital and when was he coming home. I sat there motionless, praying to God. "Please help me, Lord," I said. "I don't know what to do. Give me patience and love for my mother. Give me strength when I answer the same questions over and over again. Give me compassion when she lashes out at me because of her fear and confusion. Give me answers, Lord, on what it is I need to do next. Forgive me, Father, for wanting to run away and not deal with this situation. Help me, God. I need your help." In a few minutes, the rain subsided, and we were on our way.

I pulled out of the church parking lot and looked back at the front of the building. On the slope of the front lawn were the words "Look Up to Jesus." They were laid out in big rock letters. I whispered to myself, "I'm looking, Jesus. I'm trying to keep my eyes on you, Lord. Please help me to look up to you."

As I drove along, an old Baptist hymn came to my mind. "Turn your eyes upon Jesus. Look full in His wonderful face. And the things of earth will grow strangely dim in the light of His glory and grace…"

We made it to the hospital and had a good visit with Roy. We stayed until evening because the line of storms had continued most of the day. Momma kissed Roy goodbye, and we headed back home. As we got closer to the little town, I spotted a faint fragment of a rainbow in the sky. We exited the highway and drove onto the four-lane lined with fast food, gas stations, and micro-hotels. I looked up and there was the full arch of the rainbow shining brightly before me. All of the colors were so vivid. The brilliance of the sun peeking through made the clouds and the rainbow glisten. It seemed to stretch from one side of the small town to the other. We drove in awe of the beautiful sight before us. I knew that God was in control, and that He saw me in my storm.

God promises that He will never leave us, nor forsake us. He is with us in our storms. I knew that God heard my prayer. I knew that He loved me and Momma. I knew that He forgave me for wanting to run away and hide from life's circumstances. I knew that He would be with us in this journey.

My mind faded back in that moment to my dear friend Evelyn. She would have had a story to tell about the big rock letters that said "Look Up to Jesus" and the beautiful rainbow. My dear friend Evelyn was always a blessing to me and good at sharing her recipes for the heart.

CHAPTER 2

Celebrating God's Love

I was twelve years old when Mrs. Wallace started sharing her recipes for the heart with me. Mrs. Evelyn Wallace was our neighbor next door. She had been a widow for many years and she lived alone. She was never able to have children, so she loved all the children who came into her life, including myself. Although Mrs. Wallace was elderly, she was still very beautiful to me. I think that it was because she was always smiling and laughing.

My family had moved next door to Mrs. Wallace the summer before. I lived with my Momma, my baby sister, Daisy, and my stepdad, Roy. My stepdad worked hard, and he was gone out of town a lot. Most of the time, it was me, Momma, and Daisy.

My adventures with Mrs. Wallace started the summer after I turned twelve. She came over to our house one day and asked my Momma if I could do some work for her a couple of days a week. She said that she just couldn't do as much as she used to. My Momma said sure and gladly volunteered my services. Although Mrs. Wallace offered to pay me, I was less than excited. It was summer after all, and I had other plans. There were friends to talk to on the telephone, television shows to enjoy, and days of swimming at the city pool.

Mrs. Wallace told Momma that she would pay me three dollars and fifty cents per hour, and that I needed to report to her the next morning at 9 a.m. sharp. I battled and pleaded with my Momma, but she wouldn't budge. She told me that this summer job would be good for me. It would get me out of the house and off her telephone!

The next morning, my Momma woke me up at 8:30 a.m. She woke me again at eight forty and eight fifty. Finally, at eight fifty-five, she threw back my covers and shook my shoulder saying, "Lily, you have only five minutes to get ready. Please don't keep Mrs. Wallace waiting on your first day at work." I jumped out of bed and ran into the bathroom, splashing cold water on my face and giving my teeth a quick scrub. I threw on some clothes, brushed my hair, and ran out the door.

As I climbed the steps of Mrs. Wallace's porch, I was greeted by her cat Mildred. She was a big fat black cat with pretty green eyes. Mildred meowed and rubbed against my leg.

I knocked on the door, and Mrs. Wallace came running to let me in. Her eyes squinted as she smiled and told me to come inside. When I walked into the foyer, I was welcomed by the smell of bacon. Oh, how I loved bacon. I still love bacon to this day! Mrs. Wallace asked me if I had eaten breakfast yet. I told her no. I didn't tell her that I'd been fully awake now for only ten minutes. She insisted that I sit down and have some breakfast before we started our work. Since bacon was involved, I gladly did as I was told and sat down at the table.

It was a lovely table. There was a pretty blue and white checked tablecloth covering it. In the middle was an arrangement of summer flowers from her garden. The table was set with rose-covered china plates, shiny silverware, light pink napkins, and crystal glasses. It looked very fancy to me just to eat breakfast.

Mrs. Wallace came out of the kitchen carrying a tray full of scrumptious-looking food. There was cinnamon toast, bacon, scrambled eggs, and mixed fruit. I thought to myself, *I must be in heaven. This is going to be a lot better breakfast than a bowl of Captain Crunch cereal!*

As she filled my plate with the delicious food, she instructed me to put my napkin in my lap. She filled her plate and sat next to me. Reaching out her hand, she took mine and bowed her head. I bowed mine too, but I kept one eye on Mrs. Wallace as she began to pray. "Dear Lord," she began, "we celebrate your love for us today. Because, Lord, your love is better than life, and my lips glorify you this day. I will praise you as long as I live, and in your name, I will lift up my hands (Ps. 63:3–4). Now, Lord, we thank you for this food that we are about to partake. May it energize our bodies as we go about our work today. And, Lord, bless my little friend

Lily. Let her know how much you love and cherish her, Lord. In Jesus's name, amen." (Now when Evelyn prayed, she almost always prayed a scripture somewhere in her prayer.)

Evelyn squeezed my hand, and with a smile, she exclaimed, "Let's eat!" I took a bite of my bacon, and then I tasted the gooey cinnamon toast. *Yes*, I thought to myself, *I'm in heaven alright! If I get breakfast like this every work day, I may start to like this new job!*

On my first day of work, I learned many things about Mrs. Wallace. She liked to be called Evelyn. She was very sweet and kind. She was a wonderful cook. And finally, she loved to pray and talk about God.

I didn't know much of anything about God. I had never heard anyone pray like Evelyn did. I did not know anyone who exhibited true excitement about the Lord. I didn't really understand it all, but her sweet love for God and His Son, Jesus, had me intrigued.

Little did I know that my new friend Evelyn would change my life forever. I was about to embark on a journey where I discovered the love and friendship of my Savior, Jesus Christ. Through Evelyn's sweet and loving spirit, she showed me and told me things about the Lord that molded me into the woman that I am today.

I worked for Evelyn until I went to college. Throughout those years, Evelyn shared numerous recipes for the heart with me. I would like to share some of those recipes that are most dear to me. I pray that they will touch your soul like they still touch mine today.

Yummy Cinnamon Toast

Cover a baking sheet with slices of bread.
Liberally coat slices with margarine, cinnamon, and sugar
    in that order.
Place oven on broil.
Broil toast until butter melts and the edges begin to turn
    light brown. (It only takes a few minutes.)
Remove and enjoy!

CHAPTER 3

You Are God's Unique Treasure

I had been working for Evelyn for a month. I liked the extra money. I still had time to talk to friends on the phone and to meet up with them at the swimming pool. My summer job was okay!

One day, before I was headed to work, Momma gave me the task of watching my baby sister, Daisy. My little sister was four years old and in to everything those days! Momma needed to make a phone call to one of her clients.

Momma was a Mary Kay consultant and worked from home a lot. My Momma loved makeup and flowers. She knew everything about makeup, but she still needed a lot of practice with flowers.

My little sister, Daisy, and I were both named after my Momma's two favorite flowers. The funny thing was the poor woman always killed everything she ever tried to grow! Momma was always bringing something new home to try and grow. Things didn't usually turn out well for the poor little plants. She had quite a collection of discarded pots stacked up in our garage from plants that didn't make it.

Soon, Momma was done with her telephone call, and I was off to work with Evelyn. As I approached Evelyn's house, Mildred was at the base of a tree. She was trying to coax a red bird from its perch. She was fast and sneaky for a fat old cat. Sometimes, she would be walking around with a stray feather hanging from the corner of her mouth. Hard evidence of her latest victim. That day, the red bird was more clever. So Mildred was forced to attack grasshoppers instead.

Evelyn came to the door and invited me inside. As I reached the foyer, I was greeted once again with a lovely aroma. It was sausage. Our breakfast that day consisted of oatmeal with butter and brown sugar, juicy sausage links, and English muffins with strawberry jam. Evelyn directed me to sit down at her beautiful table. We started off our meal the usual way, napkin in the lap and a fervent prayer.

"Dear Lord," Evelyn began, "may your favor rest upon us; establish the work of our hands for us, God. Yes, Lord, establish the work of our hands (Ps. 90:17). Bless this glorious breakfast that you have provided. Look after my friend Lily, and, Lord, help her to see your love for her. In Jesus's name, amen."

Evelyn and I sat together, enjoying our breakfast and chatting about the day she had planned for us. Recipes for the heart were Evelyn's specialty. This is the very first recipe that I ever received from her.

We were working in Evelyn's backyard on this day. The first time that I stepped into Evelyn's backyard, I was overwhelmed by its beauty. It looked like something you would see in a magazine. There was a brick path that led to a potting shed in the back corner. It was no ordinary potting shed. It looked like a little cottage from a fairy tale. It was white with green shutters and a green door. There were blooming vines growing on it and flowers all around it. In the opposite corner, there was a small vegetable garden with a white picket fence around it. Evelyn had all kinds of herbs and vegetables planted there. On both sides of the yard were trees and flowing flower beds. Butterflies fluttered about, stopping now and then for a drink of nectar. There were little bird houses on posts here and there and bird baths. Under the large shade tree was a bench and a small table. Everywhere you looked, there was color. I have yet to see another flower garden that was equal to hers.

I was busy pulling unwanted weeds while Evelyn deadheaded all of her blooming plants. As we worked side by side, Evelyn cut a beautiful pink peony that had not wilted yet. She held it up, and closing her eyes, she smelled it. "Ahh," she sighed as she breathed out. "Lily, have you ever smelled one of these peonies?"

"Why no, I haven't," I replied.

She held it under my nose to smell. As I took in the scent of the peony, I was left with the same reaction. "Ahh." I felt the soft and smooth petals and touched them to my cheek.

Evelyn informed me that there were about 370,000 different flowering plants in the world. "Now wasn't that good of God to give us so many different flowers to enjoy," Evelyn said. Then she quoted Psalm 19:1–4,

> The heavens declare the glory of God; the skies proclaim the work of His hands. Day after day they pour forth speech; night after night they reveal knowledge. They have no speech, they use no words; no sound is heard from them. Yet their voice goes out into all the earth, their words to the ends of the world.

"You know," Evelyn stated, "God made all of this world just for us."

Evelyn explained to me how God made our world out of nothing. She told me how He formed the world and made everything in it. Evelyn said that God decided to create me in His own image way back then. She said that I was unique and treasured by the creator of this universe.

I asked Evelyn how God made everything. She said that He simply spoke, and the earth and all that is in it came to be. Everything that I saw around me was created by God. He created night, day, the sky, land, and water. He also made all the flowers, trees, and vegetation. Evelyn explained how God even made all the planets and the entire solar system. He designed the oceans and every creature that lived in them. Every single land animal, creature, and wild animal was made by God.

Evelyn stopped her pruning and looked at me. "But you know, Lily," she said, "His most prized and precious creation is us. He made us to love and to take care of us. He made us to love Him and worship Him. When He created man, the world was perfect. It looked different then than it does now. I imagine that it must have been even more beautiful before the fall."

"The fall?" I said. "What fell and why?"

"Man fell," Evelyn said. "He chose to disobey God and did something that God told him not to do."

"Oh," I said, "kind of like when my Momma told me not to go in the field behind our old house without shoes. I didn't listen to her, and I stepped on a patch of stickers. I couldn't step anywhere without stickers going into my feet! It was terrible. I cried and screamed for my Momma to come and help me. She heard me and came and picked me up out of the field. She carried me back home and removed the stickers and put medicine on my wounds. She wrapped my feet in bandages and dried my tears."

"Momma reminded me that night when she was tucking me in to bed that she gave me these rules to protect me. She said that if I would just listen to her, she would keep me safe and out of trouble."

Evelyn agreed and said that God wants to keep us out of those sticker patches too. He gave us rules to protect us and keep us out of trouble. She said that when God created man and woman, He gave them a free will. She told me how He had instructed Adam and Eve not to eat from the tree of life. Evelyn explained how they were tempted by the serpent and decided to eat from it anyway.

She said that everything changed after that. Their choices caused this world to be cursed, and now it wasn't perfect anymore. She said that the world won't be perfect until Jesus comes back to rule and reign. Everything will be just as God had intended it to be. There will be no more pain, sadness, sickness, hatred, fear, or hunger. Brother will not be against brother any longer. There will be peace between the animals and man. Mankind will work together, and Jesus will be our King. There will be no more tears of sorrow. It will be something beautiful to behold.

As I wrestled with a stubborn weed, I looked at Evelyn and said, "I hope that weeds are not a part of this perfect world to come!" Evelyn laughed and agreed with me.

We continued weeding and pruning. As we worked our way around the beds, Evelyn would tell me the names of all the flowers. She cut a few of them and put them in her flower basket. When we were finished, Evelyn took the flowers inside and put them in a vase filled with water. She told me that they were for me to take home and place on my table and enjoy. That was also the day that Evelyn gave me my very first Bible. It was a burgundy color. When I opened it to the first page, I saw that Evelyn had written something inside. It said, "To my fearfully and wonderfully-made friend, Lily. With Love, Evelyn (Ps. 139:14)."

I took the flowers and my Bible home with me that day. My Momma loved the flowers and stated that she should plant some of those as well. I didn't have the heart to tell her that was probably not a good idea given her track record so far.

I showed Momma the Bible and what Evelyn had written inside. She agreed with me that Evelyn was such a nice lady. Momma warned me that I should keep it someplace safe so that my baby sister, Daisy, couldn't get to it. I took her advice and put it on the top shelf of my bookcase.

That evening, before I went to bed, I retrieved my Bible from its hiding place. I opened it up to the first book. It said, Genesis. There in black and white, it told the story about how God simply spoke and made everything. I read that on the fourth day, God made all of Evelyn's pretty flowers. God gave everything to man and woman to rule over and take care of. God looked around and saw that everything that He had made was good.

As I read on, my eyes began to get heavy. I laid my head back and closed my eyes just for a moment. The words "You are fearfully and wonderfully made" kept going through my mind. Soon, I drifted off to sleep. I remember dreaming that night, that God was telling me that I was His unique and special treasure.

> For you created my inmost being; you knit me together in my mother's womb. I praise you because I am fearfully and wonderfully made; your works are wonderful, I know that full

well. My frame was not hidden from you when I was made in the secret place, when I was woven together in the depths of the earth. Your eyes saw my unformed body; all the days ordained for me were written in your book. (Ps. 139:13–16)

CHAPTER 4

The Storyteller

I loved working for Evelyn. She spoiled me with her
fancy breakfasts. Mostly, I loved how Evelyn always
made me feel special.

As I walked to my job at Evelyn's house, I could see
Mildred on the porch. She was lying in the sun, napping
and too lazy to greet me that morning. She did manage
to open one eye and give me a faint meow.

I knocked on the door, and soon Evelyn came to
let me in. We started off our breakfast that day with a
prayer. Evelyn made sure to always ask God to let me
know how much He loved me every time she prayed.
We had a lovely breakfast that day. It consisted of French
toast with maple syrup, glorious bacon, scrambled eggs,
and big fat strawberries.

As we enjoyed our breakfast, Evelyn informed me of what we would be doing that day. With her eyes big with excitement, she told me that we were going on a mission trip. I asked her if it was a secret mission or something. She laughed and said, "Oh no, it's not a secret. It's a mission for the Lord!"

Evelyn had been baking chocolate chip cookies all morning. I came to realize, helping Evelyn through the years, that old people liked to get up very early in the morning. Evelyn had dozens of cookies already baked and cooled that morning by the time I had moseyed over for breakfast.

When we were done eating, I helped her tie the cookies up in plastic wrap with pretty ribbon. We also attached a note on every single one that said, "Jesus Loves You!" On the back of the note, she had written: John 3:16 "For God so loved the world that He gave His only begotten Son, that who so ever believes in Him will have everlasting life."

We put all the cookies in a cardboard box. Evelyn saved two packages for me and my sister, Daisy. We loaded the box in the back of Evelyn's white Buick. Evelyn told Mildred to look after things. She fired up her white Buick, whom she called Besse, and we headed to town. We turned on Main Street and pulled up to a Christian nonprofit organization called King's Kids. It was a place focused on underprivileged children. This facility gave children a safe place to come and play games, eat a snack, and hear a Bible story.

As we walked inside, the large room was painted in bright colors. There were murals of different Bible stories painted on the walls. Evelyn was greeted by her friend Kathy. Kathy went to church with Evelyn. She had a gift of sharing the Gospel with children. Kathy always had a big smile on her face just like Evelyn.

As the children began to arrive, Evelyn and I passed out the cookies as Kathy gave them a drink and directed them to the story corner. After the children were seated, Kathy lead them in prayer. She brought the children's attention to the cards that were attached to the cookies. One little boy shouted out that on one side it said, "Jesus Loves You!" Kathy smiled and told him that was right. She told them that they were all very special to Jesus, and He loved them very much. Kathy asked if anyone would like to read the Bible verse on the other side. A little girl stood up and read John 3:16 to the group. Kathy told them that the story she was going to tell that day was about that verse.

The children opened their yummy cookies and settled in to listen to Kathy tell her story about a God who loved all of us so much that He gave His only Son, Jesus, as the ultimate sacrifice for our sins. She explained how our world was broken, and that we are broken. She said that in this world, people are sometimes sad, hurt, scared, disappointed, and sick. Even though our world is broken, there is still plenty of God's beauty and grace left in it. We are still able to look around us and marvel at God's handiwork in and around our world today. Kathy told us that God made our world perfect in the beginning. When God made each of us, He wanted us to worship Him and walk with Him every day. But we didn't listen to God. We believed a lie. We wanted to do things our own way and without Him. Our sin caused us to be separated from God in this life and forever.

Kathy paused and said, "Oh dear, that doesn't sound good, does it, boys and girls? But, now don't you all worry about it one little bit. Guess what? I have good news about this problem. God has already fixed it!"

A sigh of relief came across some of the children's faces, including mine.

Kathy went on to tell us that God couldn't just leave us all in this brokenness and separation. He loves us too much! So, Jesus, God's Son, came to us in human flesh, and He lived a perfect and sinless life. Jesus came and rescued us. He died on the cross for our sins. God raised Him from the dead, so now our relationship can be restored with God. We can talk with God every day, and we will be with Him forever. All that we must do is to believe that Jesus is God's Son, and that He died and was raised from the dead for our sins. We need to ask Jesus to rescue us and turn away from our sins. We must recognize Jesus as Lord and decide to follow Him.

We will still fail sometimes and sin. But all we must do is tell God that we are sorry and ask Him to forgive us. God's Spirit (the Holy Spirit), which will live in us after we accept Jesus as Savior and Lord of our lives, will help us.

Kathy answered questions after the story and gave the children a little booklet with the Gospel story and scriptures to take home to their parents.

She handed a booklet to me. Smiling, she tilted her head and asked me if I enjoyed the story. I told her yes and thanked her for the booklet. Kathy asked me if I ever came to church with Evelyn. I said not yet, but that she had asked me a few times. She said that she taught Sunday school for girls my age, and that she would love to have me come to her class sometime. I said that I would like that.

We bid Kathy goodbye, and drove back to Evelyn's house. As we drove along, Evelyn asked me how I liked Kathy's story. I told her that I liked it a lot. I told her that Kathy had invited me to her Sunday school class. Evelyn said that she thought that I would love it. I asked Evelyn if she would mind taking me on Sunday. She exclaimed that she would be honored to take me.

I told Evelyn how I had been thinking about the fall of man and how Jesus wants all of us to come to Him and receive His gift of salvation. I expressed how I would really like to accept Him as my Savior and receive His lovely gift of eternal life. Evelyn's eyes got all misty as she smiled and asked me if I would like to do that very thing when we arrived back at her house. I said that sounded like a great idea. When we pulled into the driveway, Mildred was waiting for us on the porch. She stretched and meowed as we made our way up the steps. She followed us in and sat in Evelyn's window seat on her favorite cushion in the sun.

Evelyn directed me to the kitchen table. She opened her Bible and started sharing passages from the book of Romans. She wanted me to fully understand my decision. Evelyn read Romans 3:10, which says, "There is no one righteous, not even one." Evelyn explained to me that in God's perfect eyes, none of us are righteous or good. But because He loves us so much, He sent His Son, Jesus, to cover our unrighteousness by shedding His blood on the cross. When we have faith in Jesus and believe in Him as our Lord and Savior, then we are made righteous before God.

Next, Evelyn read Romans 3:23 that says, "For all have sinned and fall short of the glory of God, and are all justified freely by His grace through, redemption that came by Christ Jesus." Evelyn explained to me that the first step was to admit that I was a sinner and separated from God, which is spiritual death.

Third, she read Romans 6:23, which says, "For the wages of sin is death, but the gift of God is eternal life in Christ Jesus our Lord."

Evelyn held up the tag on my package of cookies and read John 3:16. She told me that I only needed to believe that Jesus Christ is God's Son and receive my gift of forgiveness from sin. She told me that God loves all of us and wants to save us, although we have done nothing to deserve it. Evelyn told me that I needed to confess my faith in Jesus as Savior and Lord of my life. Then, she read Romans 10:9, which says, "If you declare with your mouth, 'Jesus is Lord', and believe in your heart that God raised Him from the dead, you will be saved."

I told Evelyn that I wanted Jesus to be my Savior. So Evelyn took my hands and we prayed. I repeated these words as Evelyn spoke them. "God, I know that I'm a sinner, and I don't want to be separated from you any longer. And, Lord, I believe that Jesus is your Son, and that He died on the cross for my sins and was raised from the dead. Jesus, I confess you as my Savior and Lord. In your name I pray, amen."

As I lifted my head, I saw tears flowing down from Evelyn's cheeks. She hugged me and told me that I had just made the best and most important decision of my life. Evelyn was right, and I will never forget that day. I can remember it so vividly as I sat at Evelyn's kitchen table with the blue and white checked table cloth. The Holy Spirit was tenderly speaking to me and convicting my heart. Evelyn, with her love for me, showed me the scriptures and shared with me how to know Jesus as my Lord and Savior. Now, isn't that a recipe for the heart to savor and enjoy! What a wonderful recipe to share with others over and over again.

My Momma agreed to let me join Evelyn's church and be baptized. I did and I started attending Kathy's Sunday school class. If Evelyn and Kathy had not shared that special recipe for the heart with me all those years ago, there's no telling where I would be today. I thank God for sending them to me.

French Toast

2 eggs
Dash of salt
1 tsp. cinnamon
1/2 tsp. vanilla
2 tbsp. milk
4 to 6 slices French bread

Mix well.
Dip bread in mixture.
Place on a heated griddle greased with butter.
Cook until brown on both sides turning once.
Serve with syrup and powdered sugar.

Chocolate Chip Cookies

3/4 cup Crisco
1/2 cup sugar
1 cup dark brown sugar, firmly packed
1 tbsp. vanilla
2 eggs
2 1/2 cups sifted flour
1 tsp. baking soda
1 tsp. salt
3/4 cup chopped nuts
1 pkg. semisweet chocolate chips.

Cream Crisco, sugar, brown sugar, and vanilla until light
and fluffy.
Fold in well-beaten eggs and beat entire mixture.
Sift flour, soda, and salt and add to creamed mixture.
Stir in chopped nuts and chocolate chips.
Drop by small spoonful on greased baking sheet.
Bake at 375 degrees for 10 minutes.

CHAPTER 5

The Weaver's Basket

Evelyn and I were at a local craft fair. Evelyn had made her famous oatmeal raisin cookies, along with an assortment of breads, pies, and homemade candies to sell. We were busy as ever selling her goodies. Word had gotten around town about her expert baking abilities. Everyone made it a point to stop by Evelyn's booth.

Evelyn could tell that I needed a break. She handed me some money and told me to go and buy something for myself at one of the booths. She told me to be sure and stop by her friend's booth. Her friend Dorothy weaved and sold baskets. All of Dorothy's friends called her Dot. Evelyn told me to be sure and listen to her basket weaving story.

I headed out on my much-needed break. At my first stop, I treated myself to a pop and some caramel corn. As

I made my way through the booths, I spotted one with baskets. I could see an elderly black woman sitting in a lawn chair as she worked on a basket. I approached her, and she looked up and smiled at me. Her silky brown skin shimmered in the sunlight. She had white hair and beautiful brown eyes. I introduced myself and told her that Evelyn had sent me over. She laughed and said, "Oh, my lovely friend Evelyn, she is a dear one."

I asked her how she got started making baskets. She told me that her Momma had taught her how. She explained how she and her siblings would always go with their Momma to pick the grasses. Dot shared how they would all pick the grasses and take them home. Then her Momma would let the grass cure for about three weeks. Next, they would pick through the grasses and keep only the tender inner pieces that would be good for weaving. Her Momma always used three different grasses to make her baskets. The grasses were all three different in color and texture.

Dot told me how her Momma would always tell them Bible stories when they made the baskets. She said that her Momma came up with the story she shares when telling people about her baskets. It was called "The Weaver's Basket." Dot smiled as she told me how her Momma loved sharing that story with others. She asked me if I would like to hear her basket weaver story. I told her that I would love that.

Dot sat there, weaving the basket, her eyes twinkling as she started her story. "You see these three grasses, darlin?" Dot said. "To me, they represent the Trinity. Now, the Trinity you see is God in three divine persons. They are the Father, the Son (Jesus Christ), and the Holy

Spirit. These three personalities form one being—God. Each part of God is equal, just like each part of this basket is equal. It takes all three grasses to make one of these baskets. If I leave one out, then it isn't complete. That's how it is with God. Without all three, then the trinity can't be complete."

"You see, there is God the Father. He is our Creator and Sustainer. We pray to the Father. Also, there is the Son, Jesus, who paid for our sins with His blood on the cross. He is the mediator for us to God the Father. Jesus is always speaking on our behalf to God the Father. Then, there is the Holy Spirit, which is the Lord Himself, who lives in us when we believe in Jesus and ask Him to save us. The Holy Spirit helps us pray. He is our comforter and our helper. He convicts us when we sin. The Holy Spirit gives us joy, peace, courage, wisdom, patience, love, and hope. He helps us to be bold and share our faith."

"Lily," Dot said, "look at these baskets. They are all made for holding things. When I weave all three of my grasses together, they make the basket very strong and beautiful. With all three different grasses, the baskets come alive and have depth. Whatever I place in the basket is protected and able to be carried. That's how it is with the majestic God of this universe. He is three in one. All three personalities combine together in unbreakable strength. They are woven together in such beauty and depth that it's sometimes hard for our minds to understand it all."

"God the Father, God the Son, and the Holy Spirit God hold all things. When we come to God, seeking and asking Jesus to be our Savior, the Holy Spirit comes and actually dwells within us. We are held by the Trinity. We are protected and carried by God on our journey through this life. The Mighty Weaver holds our hearts. He carries us through the good and the bad."

Dot took one of her small baskets and handed it to me. "Here, darlin," she said, "I want you to have this one."

When I looked inside it, there was a small glass heart lying in the bottom of the basket. She told me that was to remind me that God always holds us in His mighty hands.

I thanked Dot for the basket and headed back to help Evelyn. As I carried my basket, I thought about the story. I was so glad that God was holding me. I thought to myself, *God must have really big hands to hold all these people who love and serve Him.*

I made it back to Evelyn's booth. She smiled seeing my basket and said, "I see that you found my friend Dot."

I said, "Yes," holding out my basket. I told her that I loved Dot's basket weaver story. She laughed and exclaimed that she knew I would!

The craft fair came to an end, and we loaded up the goodies that had not sold. Evelyn let me pick some things to take home to Momma and Daisy. I chose banana bread, oatmeal raisin cookies, and Aunt Bill's candy. Yum!

As Evelyn drove us home in her white Buick, I could hear her softly singing one of her favorite old hymns. It was almost a whisper as her sweet voice sang:

"Holy, Holy, Holy, Lord God almighty Early in the morning, our song shall rise to Thee Holy, Holy, Holy, merciful and mighty God in three persons, blessed Trinity."

Oatmeal Raisin Cookies

3/4 cup Crisco
1/2 cup sugar
1 cup dark brown sugar, firmly packed
1 tbsp. vanilla,
2 eggs
2 1/4 cups sifted flour
1 tsp. baking soda
1 tsp. salt
2 cups oatmeal
3/4 cup raisins
3/4 cup chopped nuts

Cream Crisco, sugar, brown sugar, and vanilla until light and fluffy.
Fold in beaten eggs and beat entire mixture.
Combine flour, soda, and salt and add to creamed mixture.
Stir in oatmeal, raisins, and nuts.
Drop small spoonfuls of dough on a greased baking sheet.
Bake at 375 degrees for 10 minutes.

CHAPTER 6

When You Are Wearing the Wrong Clothes

On this day of work, I was completely down in the dumps. A few of my girlfriends had been teasing me about becoming a Christian and attending church. I was so excited about Jesus, and I wanted to share the good news with others. Little did I know I would become a target of ridicule for that.

As I approached Evelyn's house, I could see Mildred hopping and swatting at butterflies as they landed on Evelyn's flowers. When she saw me, she stopped her pursuit and trotted over to greet me. I picked her up and scratched her head. She meowed and purred loudly, enjoying the attention. As Mildred and I reached the top step of the porch, Evelyn came to the door with her warm smile and ushered me inside.

That morning for breakfast, Evelyn served a delicious spinach and sausage quiche, blueberry muffins, and fruit. Her quiche recipe is one of my favorites that I still make to this day. As we sat down to eat, Evelyn started us off with a prayer. "Dear, Heavenly Father, thank you for your love and care for us. Thank you for Lily. Lord, always help her to remember how you cherish her so. Help us this day, Father, since we are holy and dearly loved by you, to always clothe ourselves in the right way. May we always clothe ourselves with compassion, kindness, humility, gentleness, and patience (Col. 3:12). In Jesus's name, amen."

As we ate our breakfast together, Evelyn could see that I was a little forlorn. She asked me what was wrong. I told her about some of my friends not accepting the good news about Jesus becoming my Savior, and that I was ridiculed for sharing my experience. Evelyn put down her fork and looked at me with her kind and caring eyes. "Lily," she said, "don't let that bother you one little bit. You see, sweetie, those girls have a wardrobe problem! They are wearing the wrong clothes. I don't mean actual clothes. I mean spiritual clothes. These girls don't know Jesus as their Lord and Savior. Therefore, they are running around in dirty, torn, and tattered rags."

When I pictured the girls running around in rags, I giggled to myself at the thought of it.

Evelyn told me that in Colossians 3:12–14, we are told,

> As God's chosen people, holy and dearly loved, clothe yourselves with compassion, kindness, humility, gentleness and patience. Bear with each other and forgive one another if any of you has a grievance against someone. Forgive as the Lord forgave you. And over all these virtues put on love, which binds them all together in perfect unity.

"Now," Evelyn stated, "this is a good lesson for you to learn early, Lily. Some people just will not accept what you have to say about the Gospel of Christ. Don't take it personally, but instead, pray earnestly for them to listen to the Holy Spirit speaking to them. In the meantime, you just keep yourself clothed in the right things. In Galatians 5:22, scripture tells us,

> The fruit of the Spirit is love, joy, peace, forbearance, kindness, goodness, faithfulness, gentleness and self-control."

"We are also told in Galatians 5:25,

> Since we live by the Spirit, let us keep in step with the Spirit."

"You know, Lily," Evelyn said, "the Holy Spirit will never lead you wrong when you listen to Him. In 1 Peter 3:13–16," Evelyn said, "we are given some good advice. We are told,

Who is going to harm you if you are eager to do good? But even if you should suffer for what is right, you are blessed. Do not fear their threat; do not be frightened. But in your hearts revere Christ as the Lord. Always be prepared to give an answer to everyone who asks you to give the reason for the hope that you have. But do this with gentleness and respect, keeping a clear conscience, so that those who speak maliciously against your good behavior in Christ may be ashamed of their slander."

"You see, Lily," Evelyn said, "followers of Christ have always, and will always, have trouble with nonbelievers giving them a hard time. But God tells us that we are blessed in our suffering. So you just keep your chin up and keep wearing the right clothes!"

I laughed at Evelyn as she smiled at me, straightening her collar and pushing up her sleeves in her usual dramatic way. I loved how she always made my problems so easy to see and understand. I decided not to become rattled when the other girls teased me. Instead, I thought to myself, *They are causing me to receive blessings. Bless their silly little hearts.*

From that day forward, I looked at my friends differently. I looked at them standing before me in their tattered and torn rags. I prayed for God to cause them to see that they needed a wardrobe change in their own hearts. I also made a more conscious effort to clothe myself in the right things: compassion, kindness, humility, gentleness, and patience. Nothing is worse in this life than a believer and follower of Christ forgetting who and what they are by not clothing themselves daily in these things.

Spinach Quiche

1 9-inch deep-dish frozen pie shell
1 1/2 cups shredded Monterey Jack or Swiss cheese
1/2 lb. mild pork sausage
1/2 cup stuffing mix or seasoned bread crumbs
1/2 of a 10-oz. pkg. frozen chopped spinach, thawed
3 eggs, beaten
1 1/2 cup whole milk or cream

Preheat oven to 350 degrees.
Place piecrust in a 9-inch-deep pie dish.
Trim off any excess edges and flute the edges.
Line the inside of the piecrust with parchment paper and fill with pie weights or dry pinto beans. Make sure they are up against the sides of the piecrust and along the bottom.
Bake crust for about 20 minutes.
Remove weights and bake another 5 to 10 minutes.
Remove from oven.
Sprinkle shredded cheese on sides and bottom of hot crust and set aside.
Brown sausage and drain off grease.
Mix sausage, spinach, and stuffing together and place in piedish.

Combine eggs and milk.
Pour over sausage mixture.
Bake at 350 degrees for 45 to 50 minutes.
Allow to cool 15 to 20 minutes before serving.

CHAPTER 7

When the Son Shines Through

It was a bright and sunny spring morning. Evelyn and I were about to tackle some serious window washing. We had just finished eating another wonderful breakfast. Evelyn made homemade cinnamon rolls with lots of gooey icing. She had bacon and scrambled eggs also.

After breakfast, I helped Evelyn with the dishes, and we headed outside. Evelyn and I worked our way around her house, removing all the window screens. We washed them off and scrubbed away all the winter dirt, leaving them in the sun to dry.

Next, we started on the windows. We washed and wiped away all the dirt and cobwebs on the outside windows. When all the outside windows were done, we took our cleaning supplies inside. As we stepped inside,

Mildred followed us in and plopped herself on her favorite pillow on the window seat. She was ready for her mid-day nap. She curled herself into a ball, but she kept opening one eye to check on us from time to time.

I cleaned and scrubbed the first window. As I stepped back to observe my hard work, I was very disappointed. When the sunlight came through the window, you could see every streak and imperfection. The brighter the sun shined, the more the imperfections popped out! Evelyn said, "Oh my, that looks terrible doesn't it! You know, Lily, that dirty and dingy window reminds me of a story."

Evelyn's eyes lit up as she began to tell me another recipe for the heart. "Lily," she began, "in our walk with Jesus, we find ourselves at times thinking that we have things all together. We look at our lives, and we think we are looking pretty good in the eyes of the Lord. Then something happens. We are rude to a stranger, family member, or friend. We lose our temper over something silly. We become lazy in our prayer time with the Lord. We find ourselves worrying over situations instead of giving them to God."

"When the Lord shines His light on our hearts, we see the many imperfections that it holds. We see dirt and grime that Jesus needs to clean away. He shows us the cobwebs that are hidden in the dark places. Sometimes we try to clean things up by ourselves. We try to handle our situations or problems on our own, only to find that we have made things worse. When we finally wise up, we see that we need Jesus to intervene and clean us up! He lovingly comes and starts to work in us. Only sometimes, we have stubborn streaks and dirt just like that window there. At times, there are things that we aren't willing to give to the Lord. We want to hang on to them. What we don't realize is that the old habit, mistake, grudge, problem, etc., is making us miserable. Our sins block out the wonderful light of Jesus. It can make His light difficult for others to see. We need to ask Jesus to show us what sins are blocking His light."

"In the light of His presence, the Holy Spirit will show us what we need to ask God to help us with. He will tell us how we need to forgive someone or say I'm sorry. He shows us how our worry is not putting our faith in the Lord. He tells us how time spent with Him is much more important and rewarding than the many activities we bombard ourselves with daily."

"In this life, we will continue to accumulate dirt and scum in our hearts if we aren't careful. We need Jesus to wash the windows of our hearts every single day. We need Him to remove the debris in our life so that we can see Him, ourselves, and others more clearly. When we humble ourselves before the Lord, Jesus is able to come in and clean our hearts. It's so important to go to Him daily and ask Him to make our hearts clean. Ask Him to show you what needs to change so that He can shine His glory through you for others to see."

Evelyn took my cleaning cloth and sprayed down the stubborn window with cleaner. She scrubbed and wiped. As she continued to polish, the sun began to come through the window clearly. The glass sparkled as the radiant sun burst through.

"There," she said with her hands on her hips. "All that window needed was a little extra scrubbing and attention." "Lily," Evelyn said, "I'm so glad that the Lord loves us enough to give us a good scrubbing sometimes. I'm so thankful that He doesn't like us looking and feeling dingy. I'm grateful that the Holy Spirit shows us our sin so that He can wash it away."

I agreed with Evelyn that I was thankful that we have a loving Father who takes care of us.

Evelyn and I eventually cleaned every window, inside and out. We replaced all the screens and put away our cleaning supplies. Evelyn brought out a tray of her homemade oatmeal raisin cookies and iced tea to the front porch. It was beginning to turn from late afternoon to early evening. We watched as the sun started to make its way down to the horizon. It was a lovely sight as we sat snacking on cookies and sipping tea.

The sun's rays sparkled through the budding trees, captivating us with its beauty. It made me think of how beautiful we must be when we allow the Son of God, our precious Jesus, to shine through us.

Cinnamon Rolls

1 18.25-ounce pkg. French vanilla cake mix
5 1/4 cups all-purpose flour
2 envelopes active dry yeast
1 tsp. salt
2 1/2 cups warm water
1/2 cup sugar
2 tsp. cinnamon
1/2 cup margarine

1 cup powdered sugar
3 tbsp. milk
1/2 tsp. vanilla extract

Stir together first 5 ingredients in a large bowl; cover and
    let rise in a warm place for 1 hour.
Combine 1/2 cup sugar and cinnamon.
Place dough on a floured surface and divide in half.
Roll one portion into an 18-by-12-inch rectangle.
Brush with half of butter and half of the sugar mixture.
Roll up starting at the long end.
Take a 12-inch string of dental floss. Slide floss under
    one end of the roll.
Bring floss ends up in both hands and cross so that it cuts
    down into the roll.
Make 16 (1-inch) slices.
Place rolls into a lightly greased 13-by-9-inch pan.
Repeat procedure with remaining rectangle.
Cover and chill 8 hours.
Bake at 350 degrees for 20 to 25 minutes or until golden
    brown; cool slightly before applying icing.

Icing: Stir together powdered sugar, milk, and vanilla;
    drizzle over rolls.

Note: Sprinkle with pecans after icing if desired.

CHAPTER 8

Spiritual Meals on Wheels

It was a gloomy and rainy fall day. There was a chill in the air, making the autumn season apparent. Although the skies looked dreary, the earth was filled with the beautiful jewel colors of fall. The trees and shrubs were wearing their new attire and they looked stunning.

Evelyn and I had just finished our breakfast, and she was about to tell me our plans for the day. "Lily," she said, "we are going to make some deliveries to the hospital today."

Evelyn always liked to go and visit people in the hospital when she could. A lot of times, Evelyn would not know the people that she was visiting. She would take the patients some of her cookies, a bookmark, flowers, books or magazines, and of course, her lovely smile. On this day, Evelyn was taking an assortment of inspirational booklets to give away.

As I helped Evelyn load the box of booklets into her white Buick, I spied Mildred. She had been exploring somewhere that had a lot of cobwebs. Mildred was covered with the white sticky webs. They were across her eyes and on her whiskers. They really stood out on her black fur. We laughed as she smacked her mouth and used her paws to try and rid herself of the mangled mess that was stuck to her.

Evelyn felt sorry for Mildred and used an old rag to clean her up. Mildred meowed happily when she had been freed from her annoyance. I laughed and told Evelyn that I thought that Mildred was telling her thank you. Evelyn laughed too and told me that she thought I was right. Evelyn put Mildred inside the house and locked the door. Mildred went to her favorite spot on the window seat and watched out the window as we left the house. As we rode along in the white Buick, Evelyn said, "Lily, have you ever heard of the program around town for sick and elderly people called Meals on Wheels?"

"No, I haven't," I said. "What is that?"

"Well," Evelyn said, "they take food to people who are homebound and can't cook for themselves. It's a really neat program and so helpful to others."

"That is a neat thing to do for people," I said.

"Today," Evelyn said, "we are kind of doing that same thing. Only, instead of delivering a meal of earthly food, we are going to deliver some meals of spiritual food. We are delivering spiritual meals on wheels!"

Evelyn smiled and squinted her eyes as she explained to me that many of the people in the hospital were starving spiritually. She told me how God loved to send His earthly angels to deliver His heavenly messages of hope for Him. She said that we were His messengers, and that today we were about to make some heavenly food deliveries. I always loved how Evelyn made these small tasks of visiting strangers in the hospital seem like such important missions for the Lord. Looking back, I now realize that's exactly what they were. Evelyn was an angel on earth for so many people in that hospital. She would deliver God's promises and the good news of Jesus whenever she could. She gave so many people love and hope.

On my first visit to the hospital with Evelyn, we visited a very sick man. He was all alone. When we walked into the room, he looked very sad and lonely. We found out that his parents were deceased, and he did not have any siblings. He had struggled with health issues for a very long time.

Evelyn and I introduced ourselves. The man told us that his name was Kirk. Evelyn asked him if it would be okay to share a story with him. The man was touched by Evelyn's kindness, and he welcomed the little story. Evelyn shared a story entitled "The Weary Traveler." It was about a man who was traveling and looking for a place that he had heard about. The address of this place was number one Forgiveness Way. Evelyn shared how the man in the story was weary from all his searching. I looked over and the man in the hospital bed had a single tear running down his cheek.

Evelyn read how another man told the weary traveler about how to get to number one Forgiveness Way. She shared how Jesus lived at number one Forgiveness Way, and that He had a lovely room there just for him. All the man had to do was ask Jesus to forgive him of his sins and to be his Savior.

When Evelyn finished the story, the man touched her hand and asked her if she would help him get to number one Forgiveness Way. Evelyn lead the man to Christ right then and there. It was something that I will never forget.

Evelyn went back to the hospital the following day to take Kirk a Bible and some of her oatmeal raisin cookies. When she walked into his room, it was empty. She went to the nurses' station to inquire about him. The nurse said that he had passed away early that morning. Evelyn told me how she was so glad that she listened to the Holy Spirit and went to the hospital that day instead of doing something else. She smiled through her tears when she told me that her new friend was not all alone anymore. She was thankful that he would never be sick, lonely, or sad ever again.

Evelyn explained to me the importance of listening to the Holy Spirit's guidance and not waiting when He is urging us to speak to someone. She quoted James 1:22, which says, "But be doers of the word, and not hearers only, deceiving yourselves." Evelyn delivered God's message to that man on that day at just the right time. God knew that the man's life on earth was coming to a close. He sent Evelyn to tell him one last time that He loved him, and He had a place just for him to call home.

Scripture tells us in Rev. 3:20, "If anyone hears my voice and opens the door, I will come in to him and eat with him, and he with me."

What a joyous reunion that will be when Evelyn and the stranger at the hospital meet again face to face, and he thanks her for doing God's work by sharing the story of love and hope with him.

This is Evelyn's story told to Kirk about the weary traveler:

The Weary Traveler

A man approached me one day and asked this question: "Excuse me, but can you tell me how to get to number one Forgiveness Way? I hear that there is a very nice house there, and that the owner welcomes all sorts of people. It's said that He gives free room and board. And just by receiving the free gift that He offers, you can stay there for eternity! I also heard that when you live there, you are never sick, tired, sad, or scared. The owner's Son takes care of you, and He offers true friendship and wants to share all of His riches with everyone. I've been driving around for a very long while. So far, everyone that I've asked can't tell me where the house is or the owner's name, much less His Son's name. Do you by any chance know where I can find number one Forgiveness Way? I have almost lost all hope that it even exists!"

I looked at the man with his questioning eyes and tired expression. I smiled at him and said, "Of course I know directions to that house! I have a lovely room reserved for me there. It's not ready yet, but the Son is working on it. He is adding new things for me there all the time. He knows everything that I need. I'm certain you will love it there! Except you need to hurry and accept the owner's gift right away. The offer won't stand forever. In time, He will know when no one else wants His gift and close His doors. You don't want to miss this once-in-a-lifetime opportunity!"

The man enthusiastically said, "I'm in! Just tell me what to do."

So I started explaining to him about how to get his own free room at number one Forgiveness Way. I asked him, "Do you believe in God?"

The man answered, "Yes, I do believe there is a God somewhere."

I explained to him that God has a Son named Jesus, who has been with Him always. Together, God the Father, God the Son, and God the Holy Spirit formed the universe and everything in it. God made man and woman in His image. They chose to sin against God. That is why we live in a fallen world today. We needed a sacrifice for our sins. God loves us so much that He sent His only Son Jesus to die for our sins on the cross so that we could be forgiven. God's forgiveness allows us to spend eternity with Him in His beautiful heavenly home.

I showed him my Bible, and I told him that it is a book that is written by God through men that He chose. I read to him that he was fearfully and wonderfully made (Ps. 139:14). I also read to him John 3:16: "For God so loved the world that He gave His one and only Son, that whoever believes in Him shall not perish but have eternal life."

In John 14:2–4, I shared with him that Jesus says, "In my Father's house are many rooms. I am going there to prepare a place for you. I will come back and take you to be with me that you also may be where I am. You know the way to the place where I am going."

The man just stood there before me with his mouth opened wide. As a single tear slid down his cheek, he asked, "Why? Why would God let His only Son die for me? Why would they offer me their home for free?"

I explained to the man that God created him and that he knew everything about him. He knew his thoughts, his deepest secrets, all his flaws, and yet, He still loved him very much. Yet, in His perfection, He cannot look at us in our sin. Therefore, He had to send Jesus to bridge the gap that sin had made between us. Jesus is our bridge so to speak that enables us to reach God.

The man then asked me, "So where does this free gift come in?"

I told him, "Oh, that's as easy as one two three. First, admit that you are a sinner. We are all sinners and need forgiveness. All you have to do is ask for forgiveness and turn away from your sin (Rom. 6:23). Second, believe that Jesus is God's Son, and that God sent Him to save us all from sin. Jesus died on the cross and rose from the dead (Rom. 5:8). Third, confess that you want Jesus to be Lord of your life and commit your life to Him. Trust Jesus to be your Lord and Savior (Rom. 10:13)."

The man bowed his head, and I led him in the prayer of salvation. When we finished, he smiled as many tears ran down his cheeks, and he said, "Now I have a permanent reservation with God. He will never leave me. The Holy Spirit will always be my helper. Jesus will always be speaking on my behalf to the Father."

He thanked me and turned, making a beeline for his car. I asked him where he was going in such a rush. He answered with urgency in his voice, "Well, I have friends and family that I need to tell how to make a reservation! And who knows, I might encounter weary strangers along the way who are looking for directions to number one Forgiveness Way! I have good news to tell before God's offer expires!" As he opened his car door, he waved and said, "I'll see you at the Father's house sometime."

I smiled and said, "Okay, I'll be looking for you friend."

I waved goodbye and said a prayer for my new brother in Christ. I also thanked our sweet Lord for my reserved room in heaven. As I turned to go inside, I looked and saw another car coming down the road. I thought to myself, *I wonder whose house that person is looking for? I hope that they have found God and they have their reservation.*

Jesus tells us this: "Come to me all you who are weary and burdened, and I will give you rest" (Matt. 11:28).

CHAPTER 9

Fighting Battles with a Butter Knife

E velyn had given me the task of helping her polish her silverware. But before we could get started, Evelyn made me a special breakfast. That day, we enjoyed fried eggs, bacon, and waffles covered in butter and warm syrup. Evelyn started our breakfast with a lovely prayer. "Dear, Lord," she began, "bless this bounty before us. Thank you for your unending kindness. I know we don't deserve it, Lord. I praise your name for not giving up on us. In the morning, Lord, you hear our voices; in the morning we lay our requests before you and wait expectantly (Ps. 4:3.) Thank you for this day and my friend Lily. Help her to know how much you, Lord, the maker of this universe, love her. In Jesus's name, amen."

As we ate our breakfast, Evelyn told me about how Mildred had hopped in the back of the neighbor's truck the day before and took a ride with him to town. When he stopped at the gas station, he saw her sitting wide-eyed in the bed of the truck, meowing loudly. Luckily, he was able to get her into the cab of the truck and back safely to Evelyn. She told me that she took him some of her famous oatmeal raisin cookies as a thank you for rescuing Mildred. Evelyn told me that was the third time that Mildred had hitched a ride to town with him.

Breakfast was over, and it was time to get to work. Evelyn had all her silverware laid out on her dining room table. We covered the items with the putty-like silver polish. As we continued to rub in the polish, the tarnished silverware became shiny and bright once again.

I was in charge of the knives. As I polished away, Evelyn picked up a knife and examined it and told me what a fine job I was doing. She told me that it reminded her of a story. I never knew what to expect when Evelyn started one of her stories. I did know that I would usually learn a lesson from it.

"Lily," Evelyn said, "did you know that people go through life a lot of the time trying to fight their battles with a butter knife when they should be using a sword? Do you know what kind of sword I'm talking about?" asked Evelyn.

"Is it a big sword like the knights fought with a long time ago?" I asked.

"Oh no," said Evelyn. "It's the sword of the Spirit. Do you know what that is?"

"No, I don't," I said.

"Well," said Evelyn, "the sword of the Spirit is our Bible. When we have it and use it, it's a powerful weapon against all kinds of things that we face. In Ephesians 6:13–18, we are told of an entire suit of armor that we are supposed to put on. One of those pieces is the sword of the Spirit or the Word of God. In it is everything we need to fight our daily battles. Without the knowledge of what our Bible says, when hard times come, we are left to fight these battles all alone. Without the written Word of God, being read and remembered, we might as well be fighting our daily battles with one of these butter knives.

"You know, Lily, that God's promises are true. His Word is true. God sent His love to us in His Word. When we read the Bible, we are strengthened. We are encouraged. It gives us hope. We are told that our future with Him is the best thing yet to come. We have peace in this world of heartbreak and turmoil."

Evelyn gave me a challenge that day. She challenged me to start at the beginning of my Bible with the goal of reading it to the end. She said that it might take me a while, but that it would be worth it. She told me that when you read the Bible in its entirety, you are able to see the big picture. It tells of God's plan from the beginning to the end. It tells us how God expects us to live a life that is pleasing to Him.

In the Bible, we are given examples of many imperfect people that God used. God's Word shows us that even though we do fail sometimes, we are still loved by God. Even though we sometimes suffer the consequences of our actions, the Lord is a gracious God of second and third chances.

We finished our task of polishing all the silverware. As we were putting it away, we heard a faint knock on the front door. Evelyn went to see who it was. I heard her laughing and thanking someone for the beautiful flowers. I stepped into the foyer to see who it was. It was my little sister, Daisy. She had picked a handful of flowers from Evelyn's front flower bed and brought them to her. Daisy was so proud of herself.

Evelyn brought Daisy and the flowers inside. I made a phone call to Momma and told her that Daisy had escaped and picked Evelyn's flowers. Momma was relieved to know that Daisy was okay and told me to tell Evelyn that she was sorry. I told Momma that I would bring Daisy back with me when I was done helping Evelyn.

When I hung up the phone, I found Evelyn and Daisy in the kitchen. Evelyn had given Daisy an oatmeal raisin cookie and some milk. She was putting her flowers is a vase and thanking Daisy for her beautiful bouquet. Daisy smiled as she enjoyed her cookie. When Daisy was finished with her snack, I gathered her up and headed home.

When we stepped outside, I spotted Mildred sniffing around the neighbor's truck. I called her over and put her on the porch. I patted her head and told her that she shouldn't take any more trips to town. I took Daisy by the hand and patted her on the head too. I told her she should not sneak away from Momma, and she should not pick any more of Evelyn's flowers. Daisy giggled and said, "Okay, Sissy."

I knew that she didn't mean it, but I couldn't help smiling at her anyway.

The Armor of God

Therefore put on the full armor of God, so that when the day of evil comes, you may be able to stand your ground, and after you have done everything, to stand. Stand firm then, with the belt of truth buckled around your waist, with the breastplate of righteousness in place, and with your feet fitted with readiness that comes from the gospel of peace. In addition to all this, take up the shield of faith, with which you can extinguish all the flaming arrows of the evil one. Take the helmet of salvation and the sword of the Spirit, which is the word of God. And pray in the Spirit on all occasions with all kinds of prayers and requests. (Eph. 6:13–18)

Everyday Waffles

1 1/3 cups sifted all-purpose flour
3 tsp. baking powder
1/2 tsp. salt
2 beaten egg yolks
1 1/4 cup milk
1/2 cup oil
2 stiffly beaten egg whites

Combine flour, baking powder, and salt in a bowl.
In a separate bowl, combine egg yolks, milk, and oil.
Add wet mixture to dry mixture and stir together.
Fold in egg whites.
Pour a thin layer onto a hot and greased waffle iron.
Cook until golden brown.

CHAPTER 10

The Tea Party

E very summer, Evelyn would have her annual ladies'
tea. This was the summer that I turned fourteen. She
had asked me to attend the tea.

I had been helping Evelyn for weeks in preparation
for the tea. We went through recipes and planned a menu.
Evelyn wanted everything to be just right. We decided
on chicken salad sandwiches, fresh spinach salad with
homemade sweet dressing, Evelyn's homemade bread and
butter pickles and thumbprint cookies. We decorated the
tables with Evelyn's finest linens. She even used her special china pieces with the purple hand-painted violets on
them. We picked some of Evelyn's fragrant roses, daisies,
lilies, and ivy. She arranged the flowers and sat them in
the middle of the table. When we were done, everything

looked just like a beautiful magazine. The house was filled with the lovely scent of roses and lilies.

Evelyn sent me home to get cleaned up and changed before the party started. Momma had bought me a new dress for the occasion. It was a white sundress with little pink roses on it. Momma came into my room, carrying her makeup bag filled with Mary Kay. She had me sit on the end of my bed as she put mascara, blush, and a little pink lip gloss on me. She stepped back and admired her work. Smiling, she told me that I looked lovely. I curled my long brown hair and sprayed it with a little hair spray. Slipping into my new sandals, I kissed Momma goodbye.

I headed over to Evelyn's house to help her with the final touches. As I reached the porch, Mildred meowed, licking her paws. She must have been getting cleaned up for the party too!

When I walked inside, Evelyn greeted me with a pretty pink floppy hat. It had roses on it just like my dress. She told me that all the ladies would be wearing fancy hats to the tea party, so she bought this one just for me.

Evelyn had chosen a purple dress that matched her china. Her hat had different shades of purple violets on it. I thought that she looked beautiful. She was buzzing around, making sure that everything was just so.

Soon, there was a knock at the door. Our ladies were beginning to arrive. They were all dressed in their finest summer frocks. Each one was adorned with a fancy hat. They all chatted and laughed as they caught up on the latest news around town. Evelyn asked the ladies to gather in a circle. We all joined hands and Evelyn lead us in prayer. "Most precious, Heavenly Father, thank you for all my special friends that are here today. Bless each and every one of them, Lord. Thank you for this food that we are about to receive. May it nourish our bodies. Give us good fellowship this afternoon. In Jesus's name, amen."

Evelyn and I were the hostesses. We made sure that everyone was served and then we sat down. Everything that we had prepared was delicious. I ate until I couldn't possibly hold one more bite. The women raved about all the food. Evelyn made it a point to tell them that I had helped her make every single dish. They were impressed and approvingly nodded my way.

Soon, Evelyn lightly tapped on her water glass with a spoon. She asked the ladies if they noticed that all their teacups had been sat upside down. Then she asked if anyone had left their cups down or if they had turned them facing up so that they could be filled. All the ladies agreed that they had turned their cups over to be filled.

For some strange reason, I felt an Evelyn story coming on. Acknowledging that everyone had their cups turned up, Evelyn started her story.

"You see, ladies," Evelyn said. "In this life, we are to always have our cups turned up, so to speak. If our cup is turned down, then we can't receive God's blessings. All of God's goodness is wasted. Scripture tells us in John 7:37–38, 'Anyone who is thirsty can come and drink. Whoever believes in Me, as scripture says, rivers of living water will flow through them.' Isn't that a great truth that God is always there, ready to fill our cups? He not only fills them but they are overflowing! Now when we are filled up with blessings from the Lord, it is only natural to, in turn, share those glorious blessings with others. We empty out our cups, giving service to others just to be filled again by God. The funny thing is that we are the ones who end up being blessed by helping others."

"As you all know, when we help others in any way, it always seems to bless us more than it does the ones we are helping. Usually the ones that we bless will go and bless someone else. Isn't God good? He just never stops giving to the ones He loves. It just keeps growing until our cups are like fountains flowing everywhere. Just like the old hymn says, 'I lift it up Lord; Come and quench this thirsting of my soul. Bread of Heaven, feed me till I want no more. Fill my cup, fill it up and make me whole.'"

"Sweet friends, thank you for always having your cups ready to be filled. I know that all of you have, at some point in my life, shared your cups with me when mine was running low. I thank you for that, and I hope that you can say the same about me. With that said, I would like everyone to lift their teacups and toast with me to always keeping them turned up so the good Lord can keep them full! Now, who would like some more tea?"

Everyone broke out in laughter and raised their hands for more tea. Evelyn laughed her glorious laugh, and we served the ladies more tea and thumbprint cookies.

It was a fun afternoon, even if I was surrounded by a bunch of little old ladies wearing floppy hats and sipping tea. To this day, I always think of Evelyn when I see a teacup. I smile when I remember her wise advice about keeping my cup turned up so that my soul can receive refreshment and blessings from the Lord.

Chicken Salad Sandwiches

4 cups cooked chopped chicken
1 1/2 cup real mayonnaise
1 cup chopped celery
1 1/2 cups seedless grapes, halved
3/4 cup pecans or walnuts

Put chopped chicken in a large bowl.
Add mayonnaise, celery, grapes, and pecans.
Mix together.
Salt and pepper to taste.
Eat right away or chill before serving.
Serve on croissant rolls cut in half, lengthwise.

Spinach Salad

3/4 cup olive oil
1 bag fresh spinach
5 tbsp. red wine vinegar
4 tbsp. sour cream
2 tbsp. sugar
2 tbsp. chopped parsley
1 1/2 tsp. salt
1/2 tsp. dry mustard
1/4 tsp. coarse ground black pepper

2 cloves garlic crushed
4 boiled eggs
8 slices bacon, cooked
10 fresh mushrooms

Wash spinach, pat dry.
Cut up eggs and bacon slices into small pieces.
Slice mushrooms. Add to the spinach.
Combine vinegar, sour cream, oil, sugar, salt, mustard,
        pepper, garlic, and parsley if desired.
Pour over salad and toss well.
Chill for 2 to 4 hours before serving.

Coconut Thumbprint Cookies
with Apricot Jam

1 cup unsalted butter, room temperature
2/3 cup sugar
1/4 tsp. salt
2 lg. eggs, separated
1 tsp. vanilla extract
1/4 tsp. coconut extract
2 1/2 cups all-purpose flour
2 1/2 cups sweetened dried coconut, toasted
Apricot jam

Put dried coconut on a baking sheet at 325 degrees and
        toast until golden (stirring once or twice).
In a large bowl, beat butter, sugar, and salt with an elec-
        tric mixer until it's light and fluffy.

Add egg yolks, vanilla, and coconut extract and blend.

Gradually add flour at low speed until blended.

Lightly beat egg whites.

Put toasted coconut in a bowl.

Shape the dough into 1-inch balls.

Dip each ball into the egg white mixture and roll in the coconut, pressing it lightly onto dough.

Place balls on a greased baking sheet about 1 inch apart.

Press thumb into center of each ball, making a well.

Spoon jam into each thumb indentation.

Bake in a 350-degree preheated oven for 10 to 12 minutes.

Remove and allow cookies to cool on baking sheet for 10 to 15 minutes before transferring.

CHAPTER 11

That Blessed Holy Night

It was a late November afternoon. Thanksgiving had come and gone. Christmas was right around the corner. I had just gotten home from school. I was having a little snack before dinner when the phone rang. It was Evelyn. "Lily," she said, "I need your help. Several of the ladies from church are sick with the flu, and we are supposed to decorate the church this Saturday for Christmas. Is there any way that you can come and help?"

"Sure," I told her.

I didn't have any plans that day, so I was happy to help Evelyn out in a pinch. I loved to decorate for Christmas anyway. I always enjoyed it when Momma would get out all of her beautiful Christmas decorations. She had a knack for decorating. At Christmas, she went all out. Roy would always say, "Don't sit still too long, girls, because your Momma will decorate you!"

Once when he was taking a nap in his lazy boy recliner, Daisy put a bow on the top of his head. It stuck to his hair. When he woke up, he didn't realize that it was there. Momma let him walk around for a good fifteen minutes before she told him. Daisy and I were rolling on the floor, laughing. Poor Roy, he didn't know what was going on. He was a good sport and had to laugh when he felt the shiny red bow on his head. I told him that he must have sat still way too long.

Saturday morning rolled around. We had to be at the church by nine o'clock. I got myself ready and strolled over to Evelyn's house. As I walked up the steps, I could see Mildred peering at me from her perch inside. I knocked on the door and Evelyn came running. She had on her jeans and tennis shoes. *She was serious about this decorating business*, I thought to myself.

We left the house and headed for the church. When we arrived, there was a handful of bright and cheerful faces waiting for us. Evelyn flew into high gear, giving instructions to this one and that one. She put me in charge of decorating the Christmas tree in the foyer. We all went downstairs to the storage rooms and started hauling everything up. There were wreaths, small trees, fabric, angels, and ornaments. You name it, these ladies had it all!

Jaynell and I had the job of carrying up a big brass candelabra. It had a spot in the middle for a large candle and a circle of brass that surrounded it. There was a wreath on the circle and four smaller candles, which were evenly spaced out. I asked Jaynell what it was that we were carrying. She told me that it was an advent wreath and candles. I didn't know what that was. There wasn't time to ask questions. I had to decorate a tree!

There was a flurry of activity all around. I managed to get the tree together. With the church custodian's help, we were able to put on the top section of the tree and put on the angel, which lit up. Mary helped me string the lights. Then came the fun part—putting on all the beautiful decorations. There were all kinds of beautiful Christmas ornaments. We covered the tree with them. When we were done, Mary and I stepped back and admired our work. She gave me a high five, saying, "Good job, girl!"

We worked until early afternoon, draping garland, hanging wreaths, and stringing lights everywhere. When we were finally done, the church was glowing with little white lights, evergreen, and splashes of red and gold. It was spectacular. Everyone pitched in and we cleaned up our mess and hid the empty boxes. We bid the ladies goodbye and headed back to Evelyn's house.

As we drove along, I asked Evelyn what an advent wreath and candles were. She told me that it was an old Christian practice that dated back over fifteen hundred years. She said that every December, we celebrate by lighting one small candle every Sunday; and on Christmas Eve, at the candlelight service, we light all of the little candles and the big candle. She told me that each candle represented something different. She said that the little candles represent hope, preparation, joy, and love. The big candle represented adoration.

We drove along and Evelyn asked me how school was going. I told her that I was so ready for Christmas break, although I was not excited about midterm finals.

I walked into my house to see Daisy running around with a pair of reindeer antlers on her head and yelling, "Santa's coming, Santa's coming!" Evelyn decorating the church had ignited a fire under Momma. She had taken all of her Christmas decorations out of the closets and put them in the middle of our living room floor. I looked around at the Christmas clutter everywhere and told her that I needed a little break and some lunch before I could decorate anything else. By the next day, we had everything decorated and cleaned up at our house. It did look wonderful. Momma always lit candles that smelled like cinnamon or evergreen. Midterm finals came and went. Christmas break finally arrived! I was so ready to sleep in for a change.

A few days before Christmas, the telephone rang. It was Evelyn. She asked to speak to Roy. He came to the phone and said hello. As he listened, he would say yes and okay and sure. Then I heard him say what time shall we pick you up? Then he said okay, I'll see you then. When he hung up the phone, I asked him what that was all about. He said that Evelyn had invited us to go with her to the candlelight service on Christmas Eve at her church. She told him that she would just feel better if he would drive her since there was a chance of snow. Roy confessed to us that he couldn't just let Evelyn drive at night in the middle of a snow storm all by herself. The weathermen had been telling us all week about a possible white Christmas.

Daisy was so excited. She made sure that Momma had carrots in the refrigerator. She was planning on building a snowman family, and they would all need a carrot nose.

It was Christmas Eve, and we were all rushing around trying not to be late. Momma had bought Roy a red tie with a big Christmas tree on it. He hated it. Momma could see that he wasn't going to enjoy the evening wearing it, so she gave him a red sweater to put on instead.

Finally, we were ready and running out the door. Evelyn came over to meet us, and we all jumped in the car. When we arrived at the church, they were passing out small white candles with clear covers to avoid drips. We found some seats and sat down. As I looked around the church, it was even more stunning at nighttime. The soft glow of the white lights made it feel warm and welcoming.

The service began. Evelyn leaned over and said, "Now you will get to hear the entire advent story."

A man came to the podium. He smiled and began by saying, "Hope is the first candle of the advent. In Isaiah 9, we are told that,

> The people walking in darkness have
> seen a great light; on those living in
> the land of deep darkness, a light has
> dawned. For unto us a child is born,
> to us a son is given, and the govern-
> ment will be on his shoulders. And he
> will be called Wonderful Counselor,
> Mighty God, Everlasting Father,
> Prince of Peace."

The man stepped over and lit the first small advent candle. Then we all sang "Silent Night."

Next, a man and wife came to the podium. The woman began by saying, "Preparation, is the second candle of the advent." Then the man read from Luke 1:26–38. He told how Mary was visited by the angel Gabriel. He read how the angel told her that she was highly favored, and that the Lord was with her. He explained how Mary was greatly troubled by this, but the angel told her "Do not be afraid, Mary: you have found favor with God. You will conceive and give birth to a son, and you are to call him Jesus. He will be great and will be called the Son of the Most High." The man read how the Holy Spirit would come to her, and the power of the Most High would overshadow her. The holy one that was to be born would be called the Son of God. The angel told Mary that nothing was impossible with God. The woman stepped over and lit the Second Advent candle. Then we sang "O Come, O Come Emanuel."

A family of four came to the podium next. A little boy with glasses and no front teeth spoke first. He said, "Joy is the third advent candle. It represents the joy of the wisemen and others when Jesus was born." Then a girl read Matthew 2:10–11: "When they saw the star, they were overjoyed. On coming to the house, they saw the child with his mother Mary, and they bowed down and worshipped him. Then they opened their treasures and presented him with gifts of gold, frankincense and myrrh." The father and mother stepped over and lit the third candle together. Then we sang "Joy to the World."

Evelyn's friend, Dot, came to the podium next. She said, "And love is the fourth advent candle. In John 3:16–19 scripture tells us,

> For God so loved the world that he gave his one and only Son, that whoever believes in him shall not perish but have eternal life. For God did not send his Son into the world to condemn the world, but to save the world through him. Whoever believes in him is not condemned, but whoever does not believe stands condemned already because they have not believed in the name of God's one and only Son."

Dot stepped over and lit the fourth advent candle. Then we all sang "Away in a Manger."

Last, the pastor stepped up to the podium. He stated that the fifth advent candle was adoration. He read John 1:14 that says, "The Word became flesh and made his dwelling among us." Then he told the story about the birth of Jesus from Luke 2:1–40. He told how Jesus was born in Bethlehem. Mary gave birth to Jesus in a manger because there was no guest room available for them. An angel appeared to the shepherds who were tending their flocks. The glory of the Lord shone all around them and they were terrified. The angel told them not to be afraid, and that he brought good news that would bring joy to all people. He told them that today in the city of David, a Savior has been born; He is the Messiah, the Lord. He told them that they would find him wrapped in cloths and lying in a manger. Then, suddenly the sky was filled with angels and they were saying, "Glory to God in the highest heaven, and on earth peace to those on whom his favor rests."

The shepherds did as they were told and found Mary, Joseph, and baby Jesus wrapped in cloths and lying in a manger. The shepherds went away praising God and telling others what they had seen.

The pastor stepped over and lit the final advent candle. Then, we all lit our candles. As the lights dimmed, we all sang "Oh Come Let Us Adore Him." The lights came back on, and we blew out our candles. The service ended with everyone singing "We Wish You a Merry Christmas."

I left the Christmas Eve service with a clear understanding of the advent celebration. My family really liked it too. Even Roy seemed impressed. As we stepped outside, it was snowing. Big lacy snowflakes fell from the sky, making everything glow. Daisy ran around trying to catch them on her tongue.

We dropped Evelyn off at her house. She thanked Roy and told him that he did an excellent job driving us home in the snow. We were all humming the different Christmas carols as we walked inside our house. The next morning would be Christmas!

Daisy woke me up early to open presents. Our living room had a big picture window. When I walked into the room, I could see a beautiful blanket of snow on the ground. It made a perfect backdrop for our Christmas tree, which was standing right in the middle of the window. Momma had turned on the tree lights. The wrapping paper shined under the glow of the lights. It was a wonderful Christmas morning. We sipped hot cocoa and opened our presents. Afterwards, Daisy and I went outside and built a snowman family.

Roy changed after that Christmas. I think that we all did. He started taking us to church. In time, Roy and Momma asked Jesus to be their Savior and were baptized. Daisy did too when she got a little older.

When I look back on that Christmas, I know that Evelyn and the Lord were up to something. I'm sure that He whispered to his faithful servant that she needed to get that man and his family to church. Well, she did and he didn't stop going.

Hope. I'm so glad that we serve a God of hope. I'm so glad that an innocent and sinless baby came into the world and gave people hope.

Preparation. As we serve our risen Lord and Savior, we need to live and prepare to see Him coming again.

Joy. We should awaken every day and have joy that we are children of God. We should tell everyone about what Jesus has done for us.

Love. We need to love God and others with all our hearts. We must always remember God's great act of love through his Son, Jesus.

Adore. Let us adore Jesus, the Son of the One True God. Let us live out our lives in a way that shows true adoration for Him.

Thank you, God, for sending your Son, Jesus, to be born for all mankind. Thank you, Lord, for that blessed holy night.

And there were shepherds living out in the fields nearby, keeping watch over their flocks at night. An angel of the Lord appeared to them, and the glory of the Lord shone around them, and they were terrified. But the angel said to them, "Do not be afraid. I bring you good news that will cause great joy for all the people. Today in the town of David a Savior has been born to you; He is the Messiah, the Lord. This will be a sign to you: You will find a baby wrapped in cloths and lying in a manger." (Luke 2:8–12)

CHAPTER 12

God's Mercies Are New Every Morning

It was late March. The weather was still chilly, but signs of spring were everywhere. On this day, Evelyn had asked me to help her start clearing away the dead leaves and debris from her flower beds.

It was raining that morning, but I went over to Evelyn's anyway to see if there was something else that she needed me to help her with. She had a wonderful breakfast, hot and ready for us to eat. It was blueberry pancakes, glorious bacon, and scrambled eggs. She prayed a lovely prayer. "Our dear, heavenly Father," she began, "thank you for the much needed spring rain. Oh, how we appreciate it. And thank you, Lord, for new mercies every day. You have brought us through another winter. Thank you for the beauty of springtime that is before us. Bless this food and bless Lily, my dear sister in Christ. In Jesus's name, amen."

As we enjoyed our breakfast, the sun began to peek out of the clouds and the rain stopped. We could hear the birds begin to sing. Each variety had their own song. It seemed as if they were telling us that spring was just around the corner.

We walked outside and gathered our gloves and gardening tools from Evelyn's shed. Evelyn stopped and breathed in the fresh air. "Ahh," she said. "Lily, doesn't that smell wonderful? And look over there, my tulip bulbs are beginning to show themselves. Soon they will be sporting their beautiful spring garments for all of us to see."

I always laughed at the way Evelyn talked about her flowers. The funny thing is that I find myself doing the same thing years later, and my children laugh at me.

"Oh, what a beautiful day we are going to have for gardening," Evelyn crowed. "You know, Lily," Evelyn said, "I'm reminded of how many times in our spiritual lives, we go through those bitterly cold, dry, and dead winters. Just when we think that we can't make it through another day, the cold subsides, and the gentle rains come. They wash away the pain, making us refreshed and quenching our thirst."

"Lily," Evelyn said, "the Lord is always with us in our dead winters. He will lead us out into showers of blessing and times of healing. Our God loves us so much and whatever we are going through, He is always there."

We cleaned out the flower beds and uncovered the tender plants, so they could awaken from their long winter's nap. We trimmed back the dead stems so that the new growth could flourish. The warm sun felt good, shining down on us. We worked well into the afternoon. The warmth of the sun reminded me of how our Lord loves to shine down His warm love on us as He heals our broken hearts and weary souls. Oh, how we need to soak in that glorious Son shine! Evelyn was right. It had been a beautiful day for gardening.

> He covers the sky with clouds; He supplies the earth with rain and makes grass grow on the hills. (Ps. 147:8)

> Are there any among the idols of the nations who give rain? Or can the heavens grant showers? Is it not You, O Lord our God? Therefore we hope in You, For You are the one who has done all these things. (Jer. 14:22)

Pancakes

1 3/4 cups all-purpose flour
2 tsp. sugar
1 1/2 tsp. baking powder
1 tsp. baking soda
1 tsp. table salt
2 cups buttermilk
2 large eggs
1/4 cup butter, melted.

Stir together flour, sugar, baking powder, baking soda, and salt in a large bowl.

Whisk buttermilk and eggs together.

Slowly stir into flour mixture. Gently stir in butter. (Batter will be lumpy.)

Let batter stand 5 minutes.

Pour batter onto a hot griddle 350 degrees, sprayed with cooking spray. Size of pancakes will be upon your preference.

Reduce heat.

When pancakes begin to bubble on top and brown on the bottom, turn them over to the other side. When other side is brown, remove from heat and serve immediately with butter and maple syrup.

Note: To make blueberry pancakes, gently stir in small blueberries into batter before cooking.

CHAPTER 13

The Traveling Plates of Love

E velyn always had a way of making others feel loved and special. She inevitably made it a point to brighten people's days with her homemade lemon cake.

In her cupboard she had a stack of plastic plates. Each one had the words "Jesus Loves You" stamped on the front. Every time that she delivered one of her cakes to the sick or grieving, they were left with the sweet message, "Jesus Loves You!" They were also given the delight of eating her delicious lemon cake.

Evelyn scattered her plates of love all over town. Her idea caught on and others who had received the plates, in turn, gave the plates away filled with cakes, cookies, and breads. Even Evelyn received a "Jesus Loves You" plate one year when she had the flu. Evelyn brought Daisy a

"Jesus Loves You" plate when she broke her arm in gym class. Instead of bringing Daisy lemon cake, Evelyn filled the plate with her oatmeal raisin cookies. She knew that they were her favorite.

Evelyn's tradition has stuck with me through the years. I keep a stack of "Jesus Loves You" plates in my cupboard. I have taught my own children about giving to others during trying times. I even bake Evelyn's home-made lemon cake sometimes and share it with people in need.

My sister Daisy has a stack of plates at her home too. She always fills her plates with Evelyn's oatmeal raisin cookies. In Evelyn's small acts of kindness, her beauty was evident. In Matthew 5:16, scripture says, "In the same way, let your light shine before others, that they may see your good deeds and glorify your Father in heaven."

Evelyn's light was contagious. Her simple message of "Jesus Loves You" did glorify her Father in heaven. In Galatians 6:2, scripture says, "Carry each other's burdens, and in this way you will fulfill the law of Christ.

My friend Evelyn was always looking out for others. She would place the interests of everyone else before her own. In Romans 12:13, scripture tells us, "Share with the Lord's people who are in need. Practice hospitality."

Evelyn was always ready to share with people. She not only shared her delicious food, but she also shared Jesus. She practiced hospitality in her home. In addition, Evelyn also practiced hospitality everywhere she went. I'm reminded of the verse in Proverbs 22:9: "The gener-ous will themselves be blessed, for they share their food with the poor."

Evelyn not only shared her earthly food but her blessed spiritual food. Evelyn would comfort those who were poor in spirit due to sickness or loss. She would love them through her acts of kindness and words of love.

This final scripture speaks again of my friend Evelyn: "One who loves a pure heart and who speaks with grace will have the King for a friend" (Prov. 22:11).

Our King Jesus was and is Evelyn's friend! Her love and dedication to the Lord spilled over into other's lives. It left them blessed and encouraged. Evelyn made it her mission to work on having a pure heart every day. She spoke with grace to me and others. Evelyn enriched and blessed many people. I'm so glad that I was one of the many.

Lemon Bundt Cake

2 cups sugar
2 3/4 cups all-purpose flour
1/4 tsp. salt
2 tsp. baking powder
1cup butter, softened
1/4 cup sour cream
4 large eggs
1/4 cup lemon juice
1 tsp. vanilla extract
2 tbsp. lemon zest
3 tbsp. cornstarch
1/4 cup fresh lemon juice
1/2 cup whole milk.

In a large bowl, mix butter, sour cream, eggs, lemon juice, lemon zest, vanilla extract, and milk at low speed.

Add sugar slowly.

Combine flour, salt, baking powder, and cornstarch. Slowly add to mixture and beat at medium speed.

Pour batter into a greased Bundt pan.

Bake at 325 degrees for 1 hour and 15 minutes or until a wooden pick inserted in center comes out clean.

Allow to cool 10 minutes.

With a butter knife, go around the outside and inside edge of Bundt pan.

Place plate on top of Bundt pan.

Turn pan over and allow cake to slide out onto plate.

Drizzle evenly with lemon glaze.

Garnish with fresh strawberries, blueberries, and blackberries.

Lemon Glaze:
1 cup powdered sugar
2 tbsp. fresh lemon juice
1/2 tsp. vanilla extract

Stir ingredients together.

CHAPTER 14

Homesick

It was summer. I was about to head out for my first camp. It was a gymnastic camp. I would be gone for a week. I had never been away from my family more than one night at a time. I was excited to go on this big adventure. The day to leave for camp finally came. We all met at the school with our suitcases and bedrolls. My friends were going, and we were so excited to be together for a whole week! I hugged my family goodbye and loaded on the van. I watched them drive away, and I had a little bit of a sinking feeling inside. Soon, my friends took my mind off of leaving home. We were laughing and joking as we drove along. Eventually we made it to the town nearby, where the camp was being held. We all checked in and were shown to our rooms. We were staying in college dorm rooms. They were plain and dirty. But we didn't care. We felt grown up.

The week went by. We flipped and flopped. We learned new floor routines and tried new things on the uneven bars and the balance beam. The coaches at the camp pushed us all. They weren't like our sweet coach at home. They were intense and didn't seem to have much patience for the average gymnast, that being myself. Soon I came to realize that I probably wouldn't go on to compete in the Olympics. Nevertheless, I was happy doing my round offs, minus the back handsprings.

Camp was nearing the end. We had two days left. We had just finished dinner and some of the girls were calling home on the payphone in the dorm lobby. I decided that I would call and see how everyone was doing. My turn finally arrived, and I stepped up to the phone. I learned from the girls ahead of me how to make a collect call so that Momma would accept the charges. I called the operator and said that I'd like to make a collect call. She put me through to the number that I gave her. Soon I heard the other end of the line pick up. It was Daisy.

"Hello," said Daisy on the other end.

The operator said, "I have a collect call from Lily, will you accept the charges?"

"Lily, is it you?" Daisy squealed. "Momma, it's Lily, it's Lily!"

I could hear a lot of shuffling around of the receiver, and finally I heard Momma's voice on the line.

"Hello? Lily, are you there?"

"Yes, I have a collect call from Lily, will you accept the charges? the operator said again.

"Oh, yes, operator, I will accept the charges," Momma said.

"Hello? Lily," Momma said again.

Hearing my Momma's voice gave me a lump in my throat. At that moment, I realized how homesick I was. As I fought back tears, I couldn't speak for a moment.

"Lily," Momma said, "are you there?"

Finally I managed to get out some words. "Hi, Momma, it's me," I croaked.

"Well, hello, sweet pea! We have been missing you! Are you having fun? Have you made any new friends? How's the food? Do you like doing gymnastics all day long?"

I regained my composure, and I answered all of Momma's questions. She told me that they were going to have a celebration dinner in my honor when I returned home. She asked me what I wanted for my special dinner. I told her that I'd like to have charcoaled burgers and homemade ice cream.

I talked to Daisy too. She told me that she had only gone in my room a few times, but that she didn't mess anything up. Momma said that she couldn't wait to see me, and that she would be at the school to pick me up when I arrived back in town. We said goodbye and I hung up the phone.

The last day of camp finally arrived. That night we had an awards banquet. There was a dinner and then the coaches gave out awards. I didn't receive any of the awards of excellence like some of the other girls. I knew that I wouldn't. I was okay with that. I did receive a certificate for completing the camp and a ribbon for having a good attitude.

The next morning, bright and early, we loaded the van and headed for home. I was so ready to sleep in my own bed. I had fun with all of my friends, but I was ready to have some alone time. We drove into the school parking lot. I could see Momma's car. Daisy was hanging out the window, waving her stuffed dog at me and grinning. As I stepped out of the van, I was greeted by Momma and Daisy hugging me. Momma's familiar perfume and warm hug made me feel comforted and loved. We celebrated that night at my special dinner. Roy had made it in from his five-day work trip. I graciously shared the celebration honors with him since he had been gone too.

A few days later, Evelyn had some things she needed help with. I went over to give her a hand. Evelyn had decided to take everything off of her front porch and spray the floor and walls with the water hose. But before we could begin our work, Evelyn insisted that we must first have breakfast. She had made us a delicious breakfast casserole. It had eggs, cheese, corn tortillas, green chilis, and tomatoes. She served it with fresh fruit and blueberry muffins. It was scrumptious.

As we ate our breakfast, Evelyn asked me all about camp. I told her that it was fun. I also told her that I had gotten a little homesick. I explained how I had called home, and that I didn't realize that I was homesick until I heard my Momma's voice.

"Oh," Lily she said, "isn't it comforting when you come back home to those that you love and who love you too? I remember when I was a young girl. I had gone to stay for a few weeks in the summer with my grandparents. I had a lovely time. But when the train came around the bend and into my home town, I started to cry. I didn't know why. Then I saw my Momma and Daddy standing on the platform waiting on me. Daddy, waving his hat and Momma, her handkerchief. It was a wonderful sight to see them that day. I was a little homesick too."

"Hey, all of this talk of being homesick reminds me of a couple of stories." Evelyn settled back in her chair, taking a sip of her coffee and collecting her thoughts.

"The first story is about believers in Christ that go through life homesick for the Lord. They have asked Jesus to be their Savior, yet they stop the relationship there. They never make the Lord the center of their life. They rarely talk to Him in prayer. They don't listen to His Holy Spirit. They don't take the time to read His Word. They for sure don't try to tell others about the Lord. They are blessed because they are born again, yet they are living life completely spiritually bankrupt. The Lord keeps waiting on them to call, but they are too busy and self-absorbed. He continues to call them, but He keeps getting a busy signal. As long as they stay preoccupied, they don't hear Him calling. They don't seem to realize how homesick their spirit is for the Father."

"Sadly, the consequences of this causes their walk with the Lord to be shallow and unproductive. A lot of God's children go through life never participating in the relationship of a lifetime. This is a shame because they could be receiving blessings, comfort, guidance, strength, and spiritual treasures beyond measure if they would just pick up the phone in prayer and call the Lord."

"You know, Lily, even unbelievers are homesick for the Lord. They just don't know that they are. First, before we put our trust in Jesus and ask Him to be our Savior, our hearts are homesick for something. We don't know what it is, but there is a void in our hearts and lives. We usually try to fill it with all kinds of things. No matter how hard we try, it's still there. We don't realize that we are lost. We don't think that we need saving, and we sure don't want to fill our lives with Jesus instead of the things that we want. Yet, all the while, we sense that something is missing. It's only when we do finally listen and hear the calling of God, and we decide to accept His Son's gift of salvation. We step out in faith and answer God's call to us, and the void is filled. We realize that all along, we have been terribly homesick for the Lord. His gentle voice and loving arms comfort us, and we have found our true home and sense of belonging."

"When we call him, it's not like a collect call, where the person on the other end of the telephone, decides if they will accept us or turn us away. In John 6:40, Jesus tells us that

> For my Father's will is that everyone who looks to the Son and believes in him shall have eternal life, and I will raise them up at the last day.

In Romans 10:11, scripture tells us,

> Anyone who believes in Him will never be put to shame.

And in Romans 10:13, scripture says,

> For, everyone who calls on the name
> of the Lord will be saved."

"You see, Lily, there are so many people who don't realize what wonderful love and kindness God has waiting for them. They don't know that He has a home waiting for them, that will last forever. It reminds me of the story of the prodigal son. In Luke 15: 11–32, Jesus tells us the parable about a son that had everything. The father was wealthy, and the youngest son decided that he wanted his share of the estate. The father willingly gave the son his share, and he left with it."

"The son soon squandered everything that his father gave him on wild living. He was flat broke. There was a terrible famine, and he had nothing to eat. He ended up working for a man and feeding his pigs. He was so hungry. The pigs were eating better than he was. He was homesick."

"Finally, the son came to his senses and decided that he would go back home. He was going to ask his father's forgiveness for sinning against heaven and his father. He was going to ask his father if he could come back and be a hired servant. And so, he started his journey home."

"Then, one day, the father looked up and recognized his son coming down the road even though he was still very far away in the distance. His father was filled with compassion for him. He ran to him, meeting him there on the road, throwing his arms around him and kissing him. His boy was home."

"The son told his father that he had sinned, and that he was not worthy to be called his son anymore. But the father would not hear of it. He had his servants bring the boy his best robe, and he ordered that the fattened calf be prepared for a feast and celebration. He proclaimed that his son was dead and is alive again; he was lost and is found."

"You see, Lily, no matter what our circumstances, the heavenly Father loves us. He may not like what we are doing, but He loves us. When we realize that we have made a mess of things and we turn to him, asking for forgiveness, the Lord is there. He comes to us in the middle of that long road. He takes us in His arms, hugging us and kissing us. He states that 'this is my child. He was lost but now he's been found! Let all of heaven and those on earth celebrate, because my child has returned.' He takes us by the hand, and we walk hand in hand the rest of the way home."

I sat there, thinking about Evelyn's story. I was so glad that God had met me on my road. It made me humbled to think that the Creator of the universe celebrated when this sinner was found. I told Evelyn that I was glad that God was holding my hand as I traveled down this road of life.

To this day, I try to remember not to give God a busy signal when he's trying to speak to me. I also try and speak to him in prayer throughout each day. There have been times in my life when I did not talk to the Lord. I wouldn't listen either. I became miserable. Eventually I would hear my sweet Lord calling. I would call him back with the simple words, "Lord, it's me." I didn't have to tell him my name. He knows my voice, and He lovingly answers back, "Hello, sweet pea. I've been missing you."

Softly and Tenderly Jesus Is Calling
Will Thompson

Softly and tenderly Jesus is calling,
calling for you and for me
see, on the portals he's waiting and watching,
watching for you and for me.

Come home, come home;
you who are weary, come home;
earnestly, tenderly, Jesus is calling,
calling, O sinner, come home!

Breakfast Casserole

2 large tomatoes
8 eggs
1 lb. mild sausage
1 4.5-oz. can chopped green chilis
2 cups Monterey Jack cheese
1/2 cup milk
6–8 corn tortillas
1/2 tsp. garlic salt
1/2 tsp. cumin
1/2 tsp. pepper

Brown sausage and set aside.

Grate cheese.

Combine eggs, milk, garlic salt, cumin, and pepper.

Slice corn tortillas into thirds.

Spray a 9-by-13 glass pan with nonstick spray.

Start with a layer of corn tortillas, sausage, green chilis, and cheese.

Repeat once.

Pour egg mixture over the top.

Slice tomatoes and arrange on casserole.

Sprinkle with paprika.

Bake at 350 degrees for 40 to 50 minutes.

Serve with blueberry muffins and fresh fruit.

CHAPTER 15

Always Be Ready

Evelyn was always a lady of grace. I never saw her without her hair in a little bun, her face glowing, and her pale pink lipstick applied. Her work clothes were clean and pressed. She always seemed to be ready for anything. I told her that perception that I had of her one morning over breakfast. I had just stumbled out of bed and put on some old shorts and a wrinkled T-shirt. My hair was in a messy ponytail. I had managed to splash some water on my face and brush my teeth. Evelyn smiled at my compliment and shared with me how she made that her routine every day. She explained that being made up and presentable on the outside was only a small part of "being ready." She told me that it was more important to be ready everyday on the inside…

Evelyn shared how she was always striving to be ready before the Lord. Every day she would awaken early and spend the morning before the break of dawn with Him. She would go before her Father in a time of stillness, being respectful in His presence. She would praise Him and thank Him for who He is and was and is to come. She would come to Him, asking Him for forgiveness for her sins. She would ask the Holy Spirit for guidance and help. She would pray for others, bringing requests before the Lord on their behalf. She would read her Bible and pray the beautiful scriptures and God's promises back to Him.

Evelyn told me how Jesus himself always took time to go to a place alone and pray to the Father. He modeled how we are to pray and that we should do it often. Evelyn stated that she always tried to start her day off with the Lord. That way, whatever she encountered throughout the day, she was strengthened and refreshed to handle it.

She also shared many Bible verses with me about how we should live our lives always ready to serve the Lord and expecting to see Him at any moment. She told me that we do not know how many days are marked out for us on this earth. She said that when it's time for her to go home with the Lord, she wanted Him to find her living a holy life.

One of my favorite verses that Evelyn shared with me is Hosea 10:12: "Sow righteousness for yourselves, reap the fruit of unfailing love, and break up your unplowed ground; for it is time to seek the Lord until He comes and showers His righteousness on you."

Evelyn was not only a lady of grace but she was a lady of wisdom. The Lord had blessed her with wisdom because she was a faithful servant to Him. I try to pattern my alone time with the Lord after Evelyn's example. It is such a blessing when I am able to go before His throne. I try to go there before my day begins and give thanks and praise to my Rock and my Salvation.

> Very early in the morning, while it was still dark, Jesus got up, left the house and went off to a solitary place, where he prayed. (Mark 1:35)

> Be dressed ready for service and keep your lamps burning, like servants waiting for their master to return from a wedding banquet, so that when He comes and knocks they can immediately open the door for Him. (Luke 12:35–36)

> Let the morning bring me word of your unfailing love, for I have put my trust in you. Show me the way I should go, for to you I entrust my life. (Ps. 143:8)

CHAPTER 16

The Prayer Bracelet

I continued to work for Evelyn some Saturdays throughout the school year. It was early February. That winter was very cold, and we had been experiencing record
snowfall. Evelyn decided that she and her church friends
needed a project to get them out of the house. She
informed me that we were going to make some prayer
bracelets.

I went with Evelyn to the store, and we collected the
necessary supplies to make the bracelets. We bought little brown leather string, different-sized pearl beads, and
small metal crowns. Of course, Evelyn was determined
to make a lovely meal for her friends to enjoy. Evelyn
searched her cookbooks. Finally, she came up with a
warm and hearty chicken tortilla soup, butter and garlic

bread sticks, and a delightful carrot cake, which she prepared from scratch.

On the morning of the gathering, I awoke to see the ground covered with frozen dew. The ground shimmered and shone like hundreds of diamonds. It was a beautiful sight. As I reflect back on that morning, I'm reminded of how the Lord sends us blessings that are new each day. He lays them before us, sparkling like beautiful jewels, waiting to be received. Even when we walk in the cold and dead valleys, He sends us blessings. He loves us so much. Our mighty God never leaves our side. He is there with us in those low times.

The Lord Himself is our treasure. His presence in and around us sparkle like hundreds of dazzling diamonds. When we look to Christ in the dead valleys, we see Him through the pain. He is always there shining for us to see. We only need to look beyond the deadness and into the face of Jesus. He is our peace.

I made my way to Evelyn's to help her get prepared for the ladies. As I walked in the door, I could smell the delicious foods she was preparing. I looked to my left and saw Mildred rolled up in a ball, having her midmorning nap. She was on her favorite cushion on Evelyn's window seat.

I found Evelyn in the kitchen. She was humming and singing as she worked at putting the finishing touches on her scrumptious looking carrot cake. Her eyes were bright with excitement as she greeted me with a hug. I offered to wash the icing bowl. I conveniently scooped out the remaining icing with a spoon before submerging the bowl into the soapy water. The yummy sweetness melted in my mouth.

The ladies arrived and soon we were all enjoying Evelyn's delicious meal. Kathy told everyone about her latest work venture. Dot gave a report on her newest great granddaughter. They all laughed and told funny stories. For a bunch of old ladies, I have to say that they had me laughing!

They all wanted Evelyn's recipe for the warm and hearty soup. After lunch, the ladies helped Evelyn and I clear the table. Everyone refreshed their drinks and sat around the table, waiting on instructions from Evelyn.

Evelyn stood at the head of the table and thanked her friends for coming and helping with her latest endeavor. "Ladies," Evelyn said, "I'd like to start with a little story if I may. Last week I was helping out with the children's class on Wednesday evening. The little children sat on the floor, squirming around and talking. The teacher was finally successful getting them semi quiet. She started telling the story about Moses and the burning bush. The teacher explained that as Moses came closer to the burning bush, God instructed him to take off his sandals. He told him that the place where he was standing was holy ground."

"When she finished the story, she explained that when we come before the Lord in prayer, we are standing on holy ground. As she closed with prayer, that's when I saw something that touched my heart. One little boy quietly slipped his shoes off and was looking at his feet. Then he clasped his little hands together and bowed his head."

"Friends, will you join me in taking off your shoes, so to speak, and step on holy ground as we come before the Lord and pray."

We all bowed our heads as Evelyn lead us in holy prayer.

"Our precious, Lord, we come to you today in humility and wonder. We thank you that we are able to come before your throne and speak to you face to face. What a privilege and honor. Help us, Lord, to live as we should, as holy people who are loved by God. Bless these prayer bracelets, and bless this time as friends and sisters in Christ come together to honor you. We love you, Lord. I ask these things in Jesus's name, amen."

All the women repeated a spirited amen!

I helped Evelyn pass out the supplies for the bracelets. She had typed up a paper for each woman to have that explained the different parts of the prayer bracelet. She informed them what they would be making and showed them a bracelet that she had already made. Evelyn explained that they were to wear their prayer bracelet to remind them to continually pray throughout the day.

As she held up the bracelet for all of them to see, she pointed out each part that made up the bracelet. First, she showed them the band. "When you look at the simple leather band, ladies, let it remind you to rejoice in the Lord always," Evelyn said. Then she read Psalm 89:15–16: "Blessed are those who have learned to acclaim you, who walk in the light of your presence, Oh Lord. They rejoice in your name all day long; they exult in your righteousness. For you are their glory and strength."

"Oh, what a wonderful gift," Evelyn exclaimed. "We as children of God are given the honor and privilege to talk with our heavenly Father all day long!"

Second, she showed them the crown. "Ladies," Evelyn said, "let your crown always bring lovely splendor to the Lord." Then, she read Isaiah 62:3: "You will be a crown of splendor in the Lord's hand, a royal diadem in the hand of your God."

"In Psalm 103:4," Evelyn said, "scripture tells us that 'God redeems our life from the pit and crowns us with love and compassion,' what an encouraging picture! Our beautiful Lord not only rescues us from the pit, but He gives us a crown as well. I hope that we all will remember to wear our crowns in love and compassion for others."

Third, Evelyn showed the ladies the pearls. She had placed two pearls on either side of the crown and used a large pearl to fasten the bracelet. "As you look at these pearls, always stop and remember God's precious gift," Evelyn said. "He gave us His only Son, Jesus, who, on His own accord, stepped down from His heavenly throne and came down to us to pay the price for our sins. He did this so that we may have eternal life with Him in glory. In Matthew 13:45–46, scripture tells us, 'The Kingdom of heaven is like a merchant, looking for fine pearls. When he found one of great value, he went away and sold everything he had and bought it.'

"I ask you this," Evelyn said, "do you see this precious gift as something that you would sell everything in order to have it? Do we, as believers in Christ, cherish what our Lord and Savior has done for us? I pray that we all remember the great sacrifice given to all because of God's great love for us."

"Okay," Evelyn said, "let's make some prayer bracelets!"

The ladies examined the bracelet that Evelyn had made, and we all started to work. We made bracelets all afternoon. Everyone had a great time. Evelyn served hot cider and cocoa to her busy little workers.

The ladies ended up meeting several more times. They made enough bracelets for all the women of the church. It was a great time of fellowship for them. Evelyn said that their project seemed to make those long winter days go by a little faster.

The prayer bracelets were given out at their spring luncheon that April. The church women, young and old, loved their bracelets. They also loved the message that was attached to them, explaining the significance of each part of the bracelet.

It was neat to see the different women, teens, and young girls around town wearing their prayer bracelets. I wore my bracelet too, and it reminded me to pray to our heavenly Father throughout each day.

I cherish the honor that the Lord has given to me and every believer. We all have the privilege of coming before Him in His holy presence and speaking with Him. We don't need to make an appointment. We don't need to worry about waking Him up. Day or night, the Lord hears us and helps us in our time of need. What a blessing that God has given to us. He is always just a prayer away.

Chicken Tortilla Soup

1 whole chicken (excluding liver and gizzards)
5 quarts water
1 tbsp. ground cumin
1/2 cup fresh cilantro
1 tbsp. salt
2 large carrots, sliced
3 celery ribs, sliced
1 large onion, chopped
1 1/2 tsp. coarse pepper
2 garlic cloves
2 tsp. dried oregano

Place all ingredients in a large pot.
Bring to a boil and simmer, covered for 1 1/2 to 2 hours.
Remove chicken from broth.
Remove meat from bones and cut into cubes.
Strain liquid, discard vegetables, and taste for salt.
Add cubed chicken, 1 cup green onions, 1/4 cup chopped
    cilantro back to broth and heat.
Ladle soup into individual bowls.
Garnish soup with tortilla chip pieces, chopped avocado,
    1 tsp. sour cream, 1 tbsp. Monterey Jack cheese, and
    a slice of lime.
Serve immediately.

Carrot Cake

1 1/2 cup oil
2 cups sugar
4 eggs
2 cups sifted flour
1 tsp. baking powder
1 tsp. baking soda
1 tsp. cinnamon
1/4 tsp. salt
1 8.5-oz. can crushed pineapple
2 cups grated carrots
1 cup pecans

Combine oil and sugar.
Add eggs and beat well.
Add pineapple.
Gradually add sifted flour and other dry ingredients.
Add carrots and nuts.
Makes 3 8-inch layers.
Bake at 350 degrees for 50 to 60 minutes.

Cream Cheese Icing:
1 stick margarine
1 8-oz. pkg. cream cheese
1 lb. powdered sugar

Cream butter and cream cheese.
Add powdered sugar until desired consistency.

CHAPTER 17

Helping Hands

Evelyn's friend Dot had hurt her back. She had stepped in a hole and gotten something out of line. Dot was in terrible pain. If she moved a certain way, she would experience muscle spasms that sent her to the floor. She was able to tolerate the pain if she was standing still, sitting gingerly on her bar stool, or lying in bed. Everything else in between was misery.

The chiropractor put her spine back in line and told her to take it easy for a few weeks. Evelyn and her friends came to Dot's rescue. They all swooped in on Dot like a flock of geese landing on a pond. They were honking and flapping around Dot's house like nothing I'd ever seen.

Evelyn and I helped Dot to her guest bed. We put on a fresh set of sheets on her bed. We fluffed her pillows and straightened her room. Evelyn had brought a beautiful vase of flowers from her garden and set them on Dot's bedside table.

Mary and Jaynell were in charge of the kitchen. They gave orders to Janet and Sharon on what to do. Before long, the four of them had several meals prepared and in the refrigerator. They had some quick snacks ready as well. The ladies cleaned the kitchen and had it back in ship shape condition.

Kathy was in charge of dusting and vacuuming. She wheeled Dot's Hoover around like a pro. She dusted everything leaving the house, smelling lemon fresh in record time.

Evelyn and I hit the bathroom. We cleaned it until the porcelain and chrome were shining. We set out clean towels and washcloths so that Dot wouldn't have to bend down to reach them.

Evelyn and I helped Dot back to her bed. We all gathered around her and Evelyn started praying for her. Each one of the ladies had a hand on her foot, leg, hand, arm, or head as they gathered around her. Each one of them took turns saying a sweet prayer for their friend Dot. They prayed for healing, strength, mercy, blessings, and hope.

We bid Dot goodbye. As we were leaving, Evelyn and the ladies coordinated times so that each one of them could come and check on Dot for the next few days. Mary and Jaynell stayed with Dot for a while. They made her lunch and helped get her settled in for an afternoon nap.

Evelyn drove us home in her white Buick. She hummed as she drove along. "Lily," Evelyn said, "doesn't it feel good to help someone who is a part of the church body when they are in need? You know, we, as believers, make up the body of Christ here on earth with Christ being the head of this body. Some of us are the legs, some are the arms, some the mouth, the ears, and so on. It takes all of us doing our part to make this body of believers useful to the Lord and to others."

"We, as the body of Christ, work in two ways. One way is by joining together and coming to the aid of another part of the body, like we did with Dot today. When one part of the body is having trouble in our physical body, the other parts kick in and overcompensates until that part can be restored. That's what we do as the body of Christ. We join together when another part of the body is in need. We can do this by praying, sending a note, a phone call, driving them places or helping out like today."

"Another way we join together as the body of Christ is by doing our part for the kingdom of God. By that, I mean doing the things that God has gifted you in doing. Some of us are teachers while others are prayer warriors. Some are gifted with acts of service. We, as the body of believers, each have more than one gift that the Lord has blessed us with. We just need to see those gifts and use them to glorify God in speaking the truth and giving hope to others."

"Unfortunately, many believers lose sight of their calling, and they don't see their gifts that the Lord has blessed them with. Many gifts have been wasted in this world due to laziness, busyness with other things, feeling unworthy, or the lack of belief that the Lord could love you enough to use you."

"You see, Lily, you have an exciting opportunity to see and experience the gifts that God has blessed you with in this life! God will let you know what those gifts are. In some seasons of your life, He may give you one gift; and then in another season, it will be something different. That is one thing about the Lord, you never know where He will lead you next."

"I have found over the years that just when I think God is leading me in one direction, He steers me in another. Sometimes that direction is not the way I want to go. Sometimes it's a little uncomfortable or unpleasant. But in the end, it's always for the good. When I look back on those hard times and how I came through them, I'm blessed all over again. I can see God's loving hand in all of it."

We pulled into the driveway. Momma and Daisy were in the front yard. Daisy was playing on her slip and slide. Mildred watched her curiously as she ran and slid across the wet rubber that stretched across our lawn. Daisy squealed with delight as she yelled, "Watch, Momma. Watch me going to do another trick!" Momma would cheer her on as she sipped her iced tea and thumbed through her latest "Better Homes and Gardens" magazine.

Evelyn and I said goodbye. I strolled over to Momma and Daisy. I told Momma all about Dot and what we had done for her.

Daisy eventually got tired of the slip and slide. Momma turned off the water and we went inside. That evening, I was thinking about the gifts that the Lord had in store for me. I prayed to Him that I would see those gifts and use them. I thanked Him for loving me enough to trust me in His work.

> Each of you should use whatever gift, you have received to serve others, as faithful stewards of God's grace in its various forms. If anyone speaks, they should do so as one who speaks the very words of God. If anyone serves, they should do so with the strength God provides, so that in all things God may be praised through Jesus Christ. (1 Pet. 4:10–11)

> But to each one of us, grace has been given as Christ apportioned it. This is why it says, When He ascended on high, he took many captives and gave gifts to His people. (Eph. 4:7–8)

CHAPTER 18

Mile-High Biscuits and Fig Jam

Evelyn had a beautiful fig tree in her backyard. Every summer, it produced sweet and juicy fruit. One day, when I was helping Evelyn, she sent me out to pick figs. She gave me direct instructions. "Pick only the ones that are beginning to turn brown and soft. Leave the over ripened ones that have already split open for the birds. Don't pick any that are still green and firm."

With Evelyn's instructions fresh in my mind, I grabbed the handled basket and went outside. There were lots of figs that covered the small tree. It was a happy-looking tree. I nervously touched the closest fig that had begun to turn brown. It felt slightly soft. It wasn't cracked so I picked it! I laid it in my basket and searched for another. Soon my basket was full of the cute little figs. I proudly took them inside to Evelyn.

She washed them and laid them on a dish towel. She took one, sliced it open, and handed one half to me. I took a bite. It tasted sweet and juicy. I liked figs! Evelyn gave me some to take home and share with my family. The rest of them, she saved to make fig jam. That was going to be our project the next day.

At nine o'clock sharp, I arrived at Evelyn's house. We made smoothies that morning for breakfast. I had strawberries, blueberries, and a banana in mine. With our smoothies in hand, we started to work.

Evelyn had little jars with lids lined up on the counter. She was wearing her light blue apron with white polka dots. She handed one to me and I put it on. Mine was covered with all kinds of cats wearing funny hats. She handed me a knife, and we sliced off the stems and cut the figs in fourths. Evelyn put water in a pot and added the figs, sugar, lemon juice, and vanilla. After the fig mixture had cooked down and was beginning to thicken, Evelyn removed the pot from the heat. She stirred and mashed up the figs until the consistency was somewhat smooth. When the jam had cooled some, I helped her spoon it into the little glass jars and secure their lids. Evelyn submerged the jars halfway in boiling water and sealed the lids to the jars. We cleaned up the mess and I headed home.

When I arrived home, Momma was on the phone, taking Mary Kay orders. She was determined to earn her pink Cadillac. Daisy was playing with her baby doll named Baby. She loved her doll so much that its hair was coming out, and one eye would get stuck open when the other one closed. I told Momma all about us making fig jam. I told her that tomorrow I would get to bring some home for us to try.

Tomorrow rolled around. I managed to drag myself out of bed and over to Evelyn's house by nine o'clock that morning. When I walked in the door, Evelyn handed me my apron. I asked her if we were making more jam. Evelyn laughed and said, "Oh no, not jam. Today we are making my famous Mile-High biscuits to eat with the jam."

Evelyn had the ingredients all set out on the counter. She helped me measure the correct amounts of flour, salt, baking soda, and baking powder. We combined it with the shortening. Evelyn took the mixture in her little hands and kneaded it together. Then she poured in some buttermilk and mixed it around. I sprinkled flour down on the countertop, and Evelyn plopped the blob of dough on it. I sprinkled the blob of dough with more flour. Evelyn made the dough into a circle about one inch thick. She gave me the honors of using the biscuit cutter. I plunged it into the dough and gave it a little turn back and forth. Evelyn showed me how to carefully take it and put it in the pan. When I had placed all of the biscuits in the pan, Evelyn put them into the oven to bake.

In no time at all, I could smell them baking. Evelyn checked to see if they were done. She pulled them from the oven. They were golden brown. Evelyn quickly took them to her kitchen table. We sat down and she prayed. "Lord, thank you for this wonderful breakfast. You supply all our needs. Help us, holy Father, to remain in you. Give us faith that is just like my biscuits, Lord. Make our faith a mile high! Bless our sweet Lily. In Jesus's name, amen."

I took one of the biscuits and broke it open. Steam rose up along with its yummy aroma. I lathered it with butter and fig jam. I took a bite. The heavenly biscuit melted in my mouth. The jam was sweet and gooey. It was delicious! I ate three biscuits and jam with milk that morning. I was stuffed.

Evelyn sat there stirring her coffee. "You know, Lily," she said, "biscuits and jam remind me of two things about the Lord. First, Scripture tells us that Jesus was speaking to the crowd in Capernaum. He was explaining to them that the food they were after spoils. He told them in John 6:27, 'Do not work for food that spoils, but for food that endures to eternal life, which the Son of Man will give you. For on Him God the Father has placed His seal of approval.'"

"You see, Lily," said Evelyn, "Jesus is our bread of life. He is the One that sustains us and gives us strength. Jesus declares to us in John 6:35, 'I am the bread of life. Whoever comes to me will never go hungry, and whoever believes in me will never be thirsty.'"

"And you know, Lily," Evelyn explained, "once we belong to Jesus, He will never drive us away. We are His, bought and paid for. Our names are forever inscribed on the palms of His hands. It says so in Isaiah 49:16. Jesus tells us in John 6:37, 'All those the Father gives me will come to me, and whoever comes to me I will never drive away.'"

"Isn't that wonderful, Lily," Evelyn said, "that the Lord loves us so?"

"Yes," I said, "it is so great that Jesus loves us that much."

Evelyn removed the small spoon that was in the fig jam. She put the lid back on the jar and twisted it shut. "Now this fig jam reminds me of something too," she said. "You know, Lily, we would not have any jam if our little tree hadn't produced some fruit. Living our lives as followers of Jesus should show evidence of fruit. We should demonstrate our love for God by living to serve Him. In John 15, Jesus tells us that He is the true vine and His Father is the gardener. In verses 4–8, Jesus says this,

> Remain in me, as I also remain in you. No branch can bear fruit by itself; it must remain in the vine. Neither can you bear fruit unless you remain in me.
>
> I am the vine; you are the branches. If you remain in me and I in you, you will bear much fruit; apart from me you can do nothing. If you do not remain in me, you are like a branch that is thrown away and withers; such branches are picked up, thrown into the fire and burned. If you remain in me and my words remain in you, ask whatever you wish, and it will be done for you. This is my Father's glory, that you bear much fruit, showing yourselves to be my disciples."

"You see, Lily," Evelyn said, "as long as we remain in Jesus, we can be bearers of fruit. Good fruit that is. Fruit that is useful to God. We are to be useful disciples for Christ. Our gifts, talents, words, and deeds should all be used for the glory of God. So, Lily, don't waste your talents and gifts, give them back to God. You know, He's the one that gave them to you in the first place."

Evelyn sent me home with four jars of fig jam. My Momma and Daisy loved it. Even Roy tried some.

Mile-High biscuits and fig jam. Evelyn's recipe for the heart was a good one that day. I learned that the Lord is our everlasting bread of life. We need to serve Him and ask Him to bless us with mile-high faith. We should honor Him and abide in Him alone. This will bless us along the way as we bear much fruit.

Mile-High Biscuits

2 cups all-purpose flour
1/2 tsp. salt
1/2 tsp. baking soda
2 3/4 tsp. baking powder
1/2 cup shortening
1 cup buttermilk

Mix flour, salt, baking soda, and baking powder together.
Add shortening to dry mixture.
Knead into flour with hands.
Gently stir buttermilk into flour mixture.

Place dough on a floured surface. Sprinkle flour on top
   of dough.
Form into a 1-inch circle. Use a round biscuit cutter.
Place biscuits in greased 8-by-8 pan.
Bake at 400 degrees until lightly browned.

Note: 1/2 cup plain yogurt and 1/2 cup water can be
substituted for the buttermilk.

Fig Jam

2 pounds figs
1 1/2 cups sugar
1/4 cup lemon juice
1 1/2 cup water
1/4 tsp. vanilla

Cut figs with the skins on into fourths.
Put figs, sugar, lemon juice, water, and vanilla into a
   4-quart cooking pot.
Cook on low until it thickens to your liking.
Spoon jam into small canning jars.
Secure lids and rings.
Submerge in a large pot of water that covers one half of
   the jars.
Boil for 30 minutes on medium heat. This seals the lids.
Remove and allow jars to cool.
Enjoy and share!

CHAPTER 19

Spreading Gospel Seeds at Excessive Speeds

It was Easter weekend. My sister Daisy and I had agreed to go with Evelyn to the sunrise Easter service. It was an annual event that our church did at the local city lake.

My alarm buzzed at 5:00 a.m. I rolled over and hit the off button. I thought to myself, *I'll just lay here for a second.* The next thing I knew, Momma was standing over me shaking my shoulder.

"Lily," she said, "Evelyn is at the front door, ready to leave for the sunrise service. Should I tell her to go on?"

I jumped out of bed. The clock said, five thirty. I had overslept.

"No," I said, "tell her I'll be there in five minutes."

Daisy heard all of the commotion, and she jumped up too. She said that she still wanted to go as she stumbled around trying to put on her jeans.

We both threw on our clothes and shoes. We ran into the bathroom and began splashing water on our faces and brushing our teeth. In a flash, we were out the door. When we stepped outside, it was still dark. All I could see was Evelyn's Buick lights and the car exhaust rising up in the chilly morning air. I jumped in the front and Daisy slid in the backseat. We buckled up and Evelyn took off. I told her how sorry I was, and that I'd hit the off button on my alarm and fell back asleep. She assured me that it was okay. She thought that we would still be able to make it on time.

We drove over the railroad tracks and towards the edge of town. Turning onto the two-lane highway, we headed towards the city lake. Evelyn chatted excitedly as we drove into what seemed like endless darkness.

I turned to check on Daisy. She was sitting in the back, looking like a rag doll. Her body was limp, and her head kept flopping from side to side. She was fast asleep. In the distance behind us, I began to see flashing lights.

"Evelyn," I said, "I think that the police or an ambulance is behind us."

"Oh dear," Evelyn said.

She looked at her speedometer. She was exceeding the speed limit by more than ten miles per hour. She slowed down as she looked in her rear view mirror.

"Maybe there's been an accident up ahead," she said.

As the vehicle came closer, we could see that it was a police cruiser. He stayed right behind Evelyn with his lights flashing. Evelyn signaled and pulled off onto the shoulder. By this time, Daisy had awakened. She was no longer a rag doll. She was sitting at attention with big round eyes looking at me. The flashing lights of the police cruiser lit up the backseat, making Daisy's blonde hair flash red.

A tall sturdy looking man got out of the vehicle. He walked towards the car. When he approached Evelyn's side, he peered at her with his flashlight. Evelyn rolled down her window and gave him a cheerful good morning. The officer shined his light in the car to evaluate the situation.

Daisy sat there stiff as a board, her eyes still as big as saucers. I could see that his badge said officer Davis. He asked for Evelyn's driver's license. She handed it to him and he looked it over.

"Mrs. Wallace," he said, "can you tell me why you were driving thirteen miles per hour over the speed limit?"

"Well, officer," Evelyn said, "we are on our way to our church's annual Easter sunrise service at the city lake. We have it every year unless it's a downpour. We are running a little late, and I guess that I just had too much pedal to the metal. I'm sorry. I didn't realize that I was speeding. We were all excited about watching the sunrise during the service."

"We always put posters up every year all over town, inviting everyone to come. Would you like to follow us to the lake and see it for yourself?"

"Well, I might just do that, Mrs. Wallace. Now, Ma'am, I know you are excited and all, but I really do need you to slow it down. You have to remember the

124

two grand-daughters in the car with you. I'm giving you a warning this time, but next time, I'll have to give you a citation."

"Oh yes, officer, I'll remember. And thank you so much for only a warning!"

We pulled away and officer Davis followed close behind. I think that he was checking to see if Evelyn was telling the truth.

The service overlooking the lake was just about to begin when we arrived. The sun was just peeking over the horizon. It was a beautiful morning. There were different hues of orange and pink appearing in the sky. The wind was calm. The lake had just a little bit of steam rising up from it. You could hear the birds beginning to awaken as they sang good morning to the earth. I could see officer Davis. He had gotten out of his car and was leaning on it. Evelyn broke out the lawn chairs and we got settled.

The pastor welcomed everyone and started the Easter service. He spoke about a man named Jesus. He came to earth, born of a virgin. God, Himself stepped down from His throne in heaven. He put on the skin and bone of man and dwelled among us for thirty-three years. He was sinless. He loved us like no other. He spoke wisdom. He was kind and thoughtful. He lived and felt as a man, yet He was God incarnate. He had left his throne in heaven to come to us all so that each and every one of us could be given a chance to live eternally with Him.

This Jesus came so that we could be clothed in righteousness. He came so that anyone who would ask could be forgiven of their sins and made new. He came so that mankind could have peace and grace once again with God.

The pastor explained how Jesus willingly laid down His life for us on the cross. He told how Jesus was betrayed, and a large regiment of Roman soldiers were sent to arrest him. When he was asked if he was the man Jesus, he answered with a simple I AM. The power of those two words sent everyone standing to the ground. So powerful yet humbling himself for us. Jesus held all the power over the entire universe, yet He chose to willingly lay down His life for us.

The angry mob took Jesus and questioned and tortured Him for hours. He was beaten, bloodied, and bruised. Our Lord never once put up a fight but surrendered like a gentle lamb.

He explained how Jesus's body was pierced for you and me. He hung on a cross between two thieves. One thief cursed Him while the other said to Him, "Jesus, remember me when you come into your kingdom." And Jesus answered him, saying, "Truly I tell you, today you will be with me in paradise."

The pastor told how darkness came over the whole land from noon until three in the afternoon. There was an earthquake. The curtain in the Jewish temple was torn in two from top to bottom. Jesus said the words, "It is finished," and He breathed His last breath.

Next, he told how Jesus's friends came and took down Jesus's body. They wrapped Him in a linen cloth and placed Him in a rock tomb. On the third day, when the women went to the tomb to prepare the body with spices, Jesus was gone. The Lion of Judah had conquered death and the grave. He had risen just like He told them He would.

Jesus remained on earth for forty days, speaking of the kingdom of God to others and strengthening His disciples. During that time, He told His disciples about the promised gift of the Holy Spirit, that He would send to dwell in us when we accept Jesus as our Savior.

Jesus ascended up and was taken to heaven in a cloud. He took His place at the right hand of the Father.

What a glorious story of love, sacrifice, truth, and hope. God the Son came and lived. He celebrated, he loved, he worshipped, and he suffered and died for all mankind. He did these things so that today, you and I can say yes to His gift of life. When we accept Jesus as our Lord and Savior, He gives us eternal life. We are able to ask for forgiveness and start new because in Jesus, we are all a new creation. The Lord Jesus is the God of new beginnings. He can take every stain that there may be on your life and make it as white as snow.

The pastor asked us to bow our heads and he prayed, "Dear, God, thank you for sending your Son, Jesus, to die for us. Thank you, God, for loving us and never giving up on us. Thank you for picking us up when we fall, for holding us when we cry, for helping us when we are in need. We celebrate this Easter Sunday because the grave is empty. Because our Jesus lives and will return one day to rule. Thank you, Father, Son, and Holy Spirit. Help us, Lord, to love you back. In Jesus's name, amen."

After the service, we had donuts, coffee, and orange juice. Evelyn took officer Davis a donut and a cup of coffee. He was appreciative. He told her that he enjoyed the sunrise service. Evelyn gave him a church brochure that told about our church and how to accept Jesus as Savior. She invited him to church. He told her that he was married and had two children, a boy and a girl. He said that he might just have to come sometime.

I helped Evelyn load the lawn chairs into her car. Daisy crawled in the backseat, still eating a donut. Evelyn drove back to town, being very mindful of her speed. We pulled into her driveway, and I helped Evelyn unload the lawn chairs. We said our goodbyes, and Daisy and I left to get showered and dressed for the church Easter service.

As we were walking away, Daisy giggled and turned around yelling, "Goodbye, Grandma!"

Evelyn laughed as she yelled back, "See you at church little, grand-daughters!"

We didn't mind being called Evelyn's grand-daughters. Daisy and me never knew our grandmothers. They had died before we were born. Evelyn was the only thing close to a grandma that we'd ever had. So in God's own loving way, He gave Evelyn grandchildren and us a grandma.

A month or so passed. I was sitting in church one Sunday morning. I looked up to see a tall and sturdy looking man with a pretty blonde wife and two little children walking in. I thought that the man looked very familiar. Was it? Could it be? It was. Officer Davis had come to church and brought his little family. Evelyn eyed him right away and went over and introduced herself to his wife. They laughed and chatted as Evelyn, in her usual way, made them feel loved and welcomed.

A few weeks later, Officer Davis and his family joined our church. He and his wife both asked Jesus to be their Savior and were baptized. It was such a blessing to me to watch them walk down the aisle and to hear the pastor announce their decisions.

While I was working for Evelyn that next week, we talked about how happy we were for the Davis family. Evelyn teased saying that you never know how God may choose to use you in situations. She looked at me grinning and said, "Even if the Lord causes you to spread Gospel seeds at excessive speeds," winking at me and letting out a chuckle.

"Yes," I said, "you never know when a grandma with the pedal to the metal will be on a mission from God!"

We both cracked up, feeling true joy for the happy ending to our Easter sunrise adventure.

> He is not here; he has risen! Remember how He told you, while He was still with you in Galilee: The Son of Man must be delivered over to the hands of sinners, be crucified and on the third day be raised again. (Luke 24:6–7)

> Then Jesus told him, "Because you have seen me, you have believed; blessed are those who have not seen and yet have believed." (John 20:29)

CHAPTER 20

Getting Your Holy Socks Knocked Off

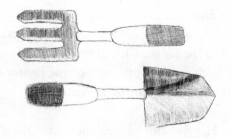

It was the middle of July. The past few days had been to use the expression, "hotter than blue blazes." I had been at the city pool all day, staying cool with friends. We sat lined up on our beach towels, smearing baby oil all over us, trying to get a tan. We would lay there until we couldn't take the heat any longer. Finally we all would run to the edge and take turns doing the Nestea plunge.

I had to bring Daisy along. She splashed around and yelled at me to watch her do tricks. She would stand on the side, holding her nose and jump in the cool water. When she came up, she would spit and cough. Her hair would be in her eyes as she dog-paddled to the edge, catching her breath before she did her trick all over again.

Sunburned and smelling of heavy chlorine, we decided to ride our bikes home. Daisy had just learned to ride her new purple bicycle with the multicolored daisies on the basket.

We rode into the driveway and parked our bikes. When we walked inside the house, we could smell dinner cooking. Momma was making tacos, one of our favorites.

I showered off and then helped Momma set the table. Roy was gone on a job again. It was quiet when he was gone. When he was home, he was always joking with all of us and laughing his big belly laugh. He was also on the phone a lot with clients. His booming voice and jolly laughter could be heard throughout the house.

Daisy and I devoured the savory tacos. Momma made strawberry shortcake for dessert. After dinner, Momma told me to go and put up our bikes in the garage. When I walked outside, I saw Evelyn sitting on her front porch. She was sipping a cool glass of lemonade. After I put up the bikes, I walked over to say hi. Thankfully the evening had turned off nice. There was a cool breeze that gently rustled through the trees. Evelyn invited me to sit down in one of her wicker rocking chairs. It had a soft fluffy cushion. Evelyn went inside and got another glass of lemonade for me.

As we sat there, rocking in the cool of the summer evening, I told Evelyn about my day. She laughed when I told her about Daisy and her water tricks and about me and my friends doing the Nestea plunge.

The sun's evening glow made the flowers and shrubs in Evelyn's yard even more vivid. I told her that her yard sure did look pretty.

Evelyn sat there rocking and sipping her lemonade. Soon she looked up from her glass and smiled. "You know, Lily," she said, "the garden of Eden must have been something to behold. When I come out here in the evenings, I look around at the beauty of the flowers and the trees. I listen as the birds are saying their final calls before bed. I watch the dragonflies and butterflies flying about, landing on the flowers for a rest. I feel the cool breeze on my face. Then, I think to myself, *when I see this world someday in its perfection, it will probably knock my holy socks off.*"

I laughed at Evelyn's expression of "knock my holy socks off."

"You know, Lily," Evelyn said, "we don't have to wait until we see the Lord face to face to have our holy socks knocked off. The Lord wants to work in our lives and show us things while we are here on earth that will flat knock our holy socks off."

"We must have faith and always be on the lookout. Unfortunately we sometimes miss those moments that God is trying to give us. Jesus wants to come and walk with us in our lives, just like He came and walked in the garden of Eden. Jesus gave us the promise of the blessed gift of the Holy Spirit. When we become believers in Christ, we receive the beautiful and powerful gift of His Holy Spirit. We just need to slow down, take Him by the hand, and walk. We need to talk to the Lord. Tell Him about our day. Share our struggles and our fears. Come to Him and ask what He already knows we are longing for. We have to believe that God is no ordinary god. Our Lord and Savior is the creator of the universe. So getting your holy socks knocked off should be expected!"

Evelyn and I continued to sit in the comfy rockers. We enjoyed the cool evening breeze as Evelyn shared her stories of getting her holy socks knocked off.

> The apostles said to the Lord, "Increase our faith!" He replied, "If you have faith as small as a mustard seed, you can say to this mulberry tree, 'Be uprooted and planted in the sea,' and it will obey you. (Luke 17:5–6)

> And Jesus answered and said to them, "Truly I say to you, if you have faith and do not doubt, you will not only do what was done to the fig tree, but even if you say to this mountain, 'Be taken up and cast into the sea,' it will happen. (Matt. 21:21)

> And Jesus answered saying to them, "Have faith in God." (Mark 11:22)

CHAPTER 21

Withered Grass

Evelyn and I were planning on working outside. The forecast called for another hot summer's day. I had plans of going to the swimming pool with friends that afternoon.

Evelyn had me come early that morning to beat the heat. I reported for weed duty at 7:00 a.m. My body felt like it was in shock. I was used to getting up at 8:45 a.m. and running out the door by 8:58 a.m. since Evelyn was just next door. I finally managed to drag myself out of bed and over to Evelyn's house on time.

When I walked inside that morning, it was filled with the wonderful aroma of breakfast. I smelled coffee brewing and bacon sizzling. Evelyn had made cheesy egg omelets, bacon, and toast with orange marmalade jelly.

I had developed a taste for coffee. I did, however, add plenty of cream and sugar to it. Evelyn would laugh and tell me that I liked to have a little bit of coffee with my cream and sugar.

We finished up breakfast and went outside. I was weeding again for the third time that summer! It was my least favorite thing to do at Evelyn's house. And yet, it was always the job that I was stuck with.

As I made my way around the flower beds, I spotted an old rusted watering can sitting in the grass. I picked it up and asked Evelyn what she wanted me to do with it. When I looked down, I could see that the old can had left a perfect circle of yellow withered grass underneath it. I showed the spot to Evelyn.

"Oh," she said, "that withered yellow circle reminds me of our souls when we keep the Lord from shining in our lives."

"What do you mean?" I asked her.

"Well," she said, "a lot of the time, believers in Christ try to live their lives on their own. They try to live on their own strength instead of going to the Lord and asking him for his strength. They are too busy for a prayer life, although they have good intentions. Reading the Bible is on the list too, but the days just seem to slip away, and it doesn't get done. Pretty soon, their spiritual life looks like this grass under the watering can. It's yellow and withered. It isn't getting the Lord's light that it desperately needs."

"Lily, one thing that is very important as a follower of Jesus is to always keep communication open to the Father through prayer and reading His Word. Without those two things, we are weak and sometimes fall into trouble. Satan, the evil one, likes us weak and unknowing. He doesn't want us to know the Father and His Word. He wants us to accept the norms of this world even if they are immoral, unholy, and unhealthy. We just tell ourselves that everyone else is doing it, and they are nice people, so it must be okay. But if we would just read the Word of God, it plainly gives us guidelines of what He expects. Even if we don't follow the norms of the world and we strive to live a moral life, a lot of us can find plenty of other things in this world to fill our lives."

"Lily, you should always put Christ in the center of your life. Love Him above all. Trust Him in all things. Look to Him first."

I looked down at the yellow and withered circle again. It made me sad to think that I could become that way when I didn't allow the Lord's light to shine in my life.

Years later, I still remember Evelyn's words. When things come up and I'm tempted to go with the norms of this world, I stop and go back to God's Word. I ask Him to make my path straight.

> You, God, are my God, earnestly I seek you; I Thirst for you, my whole being longs for you, In a dry and parched land where there is no water. I have seen you in the sanctuary and beheld your power and your glory. Because your love is better than life, my lips will glorify you. I will

praise you As long as I live, and in your name I will lift up my hands. (Ps. 63:1–4)

I keep asking that the God of our Lord Jesus Christ, the glorious Father, may give you the Spirit of wisdom and revelation, so that you may know him better. I pray that the eyes of your heart may be enlightened in order that you may know the hope to which he has called you, the riches of his glorious inheritance in his holy people, and his incomparably great power for us who believe. (Eph. 1:17–19)

Oh, how I love your law! I meditate on it all day long. Your commands are always with me and make me wiser than my enemies. I have more insight than all my teachers, for I meditate on your statutes. I have more understanding than the elders, for I obey your precepts. I have kept my feet from every evil path so that I might obey your word. (Ps. 119:97–101)

CHAPTER 22

The Prayer Group

Evelyn belonged to a prayer group. It was a group of women from her church. It wasn't a large group. It was small. It consisted of herself, Mary, Jaynell, Janet, and Sharon. They met every Tuesday morning at 8:00 a.m. sharp.

One day, while we were working at Evelyn's house, I began to ask her what they did in her prayer group. She explained to me that they would meet and talk for a bit. Someone may tell the others about a prayer concern they had. It could be about something personal or about a family member, friend, or church member. It could even be a concern about a stranger that someone had met the week before.

After that, they began their prayer time. I told her that I thought that was neat to have a group to pray with. I asked her if she was embarrassed to pray in front of the other women. She told me that the first time was a little strange just because she had never done anything like that before. But she said that even the first time that she went to her prayer group, she was blessed beyond measure. She knew that this special time with the Lord and other dear sisters in Christ was strength for her soul.

Evelyn asked me if I would like to go with her sometime and pray with the group. I must have had a look of terror on my face because Evelyn smiled and said, "You don't have to pray unless you want to. When it comes around to you, after a few seconds, someone else will start praying. Sometimes," she said smiling, "we get so fired up that we just start praying out of order and adding to each other's prayers. No matter what happens, we are always blessed when we come together before the Lord."

After I thought about Evelyn's prayer group for a few days, I decided that I would go with her and check it out. I set my alarm for seven fifteen. The next morning, my alarm went off right on time—seven fifteen. Ugh!

I got up and got myself ready. I made my own breakfast. Two pieces of toast with grape jam. Nothing like Evelyn's. At seven forty-five, I headed over to Evelyn's. She was just coming out the door. We loaded up in the white Buick and off we went.

The ladies met at Jaynell's house for prayer most days. She had a beautiful and inviting home. It was full of things about the Lord. Her friendly husband greeted us with a hearty hello and disappeared with his coffee. We walked into a little room with a loveseat and chairs arranged in a circle. The women smiled and greeted me. They told me how glad they were that I had decided to join them.

We all chatted for a few minutes and then prayer group began. There was a box of tissues sitting in the middle of the loveseat. Each woman grabbed one before we began. Evelyn handed one to me. I thought to myself, *Why are we going to need these tissues? I'm not sure that I want to cry in front of these ladies.*

Mary was the leader of the group. She began by asking the Lord to quiet our minds and to help us to focus on Him. Next, she started with prayers of thanksgiving and praise to the Lord. She thanked Him for answered prayer, for His promises and quoted scripture of praise and thanksgiving. She also quoted scripture that proclaimed His greatness, His absolute truth, that He is All-Powerful, Holy and never-changing.

Then Jaynell did more of the same praising the Lord and quoting His truths. She praised Him for the beauty of the morning and the beauty of the earth. Then came Janet, giving God praise and quoting scripture. She praised Him and called Him Elohim—our Creator—and Jehovah-Jirah—the Lord will provide. Evelyn was next. She praised God for His everlasting love and kindness. Then it came to me. Electricity seemed to run through my body. I was nervous. I did seem to get out a sentence or two, then I left it to Sharon. She took over with a prayer of zeal and excitement. She praised Him for His goodness and mercy. The ladies continued their prayers of thanksgiving for another round.

I sat there, listening to their words of praise and thanksgiving to God. It was beautiful to hear the different ways that the women spoke to the Lord. They all had different personalities and different ways of speaking to the Father. It was refreshing as I sat there with my eyes closed in agreement with their beautiful words that were being spoken to the Lord.

Next, Mary lead us into a time of repentance before the Lord. She spoke of her sins and asked for forgiveness. The other ladies followed suit. As I listened to them stating their sins, I was touched at how honest they were and humble before the Lord and the group. Then it came to me. I asked the Lord to forgive me for not being very patient with my little sister, Daisy, and for Him to help me to be more loving to her.

Mary lead us into a time of supplication next. I did not know what supplication meant. I quickly came to realize that this was a time of praying for others and ourselves. Evelyn prayed for me. She prayed that I would have strength and courage in my new walk with the Lord. She prayed that I would always listen to His voice and live by the written Word of God.

There were so many people that these ladies knew who were in need of prayer. Now, I knew why we all had a tissue. Some of the prayers made me cry as each woman would pour out her heart before the Lord. There were sick people, unsaved people, sad people. You name it. I didn't realize that there were so many problems everywhere. I did pray for my stepdad, Roy. He had to be gone so much with work, and it was getting him down. He missed being at home with us.

I was struck by the sincere and determined prayers of these women. I decided that if I had a real problem, I was bringing it straight to this group for some help!

Our prayer time finally came to a close. Everyone opened their eyes and patted them with their tissue. A couple of the women had to blow their noses. I thanked the ladies for letting me come. They hugged me and told me to come back anytime.

Evelyn and I arrived back at her house. Mildred greeted us with another bird feather hanging from her mouth. Evelyn shamed her and told her that she shouldn't kill the pretty birds. Mildred sat there, licking her paws and preparing for a big nap since she just had breakfast.

I told Evelyn thanks for letting me come with her. Evelyn smiled her usual smile and told me that I was special to that group. She said that they had been praying for me for a while now. She said that they all cried and gave praises of joy and thanksgiving to the Lord when she informed them that I had asked Jesus to be Lord of my life. It was an answer to their prayers.

Recipes for Prayer

This, then, is how you should pray: 'Our Father in heaven, hallowed be your name, your kingdom come, your will be done, on earth as it is in heaven. Give us today our daily bread.

And forgive us our debts, as we also have forgiven our debtors. And lead us not into temptation, But deliver us from the evil one.' (Matt. 6:9–13)

Therefore confess your sins to each other and pray for each other so that you may be healed. The prayer of a righteous person is powerful and effective. (James 5:7)

"Again, truly I tell you that if two of you on earth agree about anything they ask for, it will be done for them by my Father in heaven. For where two or three gather in my name, there am I with them." (Matt. 18:18–19)

CHAPTER 23

The Beauty of the Butterfly

It was early spring of my junior year in college when I received a letter from Evelyn. During Christmas break, I had gone to see her. She wasn't feeling well. Her doctor was insisting on running some tests after the New Year. In this letter, Evelyn was informing me that the tests had confirmed that she was indeed sick. She told me that she just had to write and tell me one more story. In my mind, I can just see her eyes wide with excitement as her story was unfolding on the page.

Here is the last recipe for the heart that I received from Evelyn:

Dear Lily,

I hope that this letter finds you well. It is a beautiful spring day here. My daffodil and tulip bulbs are starting to peek through the soil.

I know that you were worried about me at Christmas. The doctor ran some tests, and like he suspected, I am sick. He told me that my body parts are basically old and worn out.

I just cannot leave this earth without telling you one more story. It is about the metamorphosis of the butterfly and how it mirrors our journey with Jesus.

You see, the beautiful butterfly doesn't start out that way. It slowly becomes beautiful. It's a process. First it's an egg, then it's an ugly larva and in time, becomes a caterpillar. The caterpillar eats and eats. It keeps growing and has to continually shed its old skin that is too small. It keeps getting rid of the old self in order to put on the new self. When it reaches its full maturity, it stops eating, hangs upside down, and it forms a chrysalis around itself. Inside the chrysalis the amazing metamorphosis takes place. The caterpillar wrestles and struggles.

This helps it to become strong so that when it emerges it will be able to fly. In time, it finally breaks free. The fuzzy little caterpillar has become a beautiful butterfly with intricate features, colors, and designs that are breathtaking. It's no longer inching its way around on the ground. It's free to fly!

In our journey with Jesus, we, too, must do a lot of changing and growing before our ultimate beauty can be revealed. Like the butterfly, it's a lifelong process. As we walk with Jesus, He shows us things that we need to shed that hampers our growing. In this process, we are continually dying to our old self and putting on the new self. In order to continue our spiritual growth, God has provided us with His Word and given us the privilege of prayer. We wrestle and struggle sometimes. But with each new difficulty, we are becoming stronger when we rely on the Lord.

At the end of our journey, like the butterfly, we are completely transformed from the inside out. We emerge as something beautiful because we have become like Jesus.

Our goal in this life is to strive to be more like Him every day.

Always remember, Lily, that you are a continual work in progress. Don't get discouraged. You can't be perfect all the time. You will fail. The important thing is to just keep striving in your walk with the Lord. Always keep talking to God but also, don't forget to listen.

When hard times come, ask the Lord to make you strong. Lean on Him for wisdom and understanding.

My time on this earth is almost over, sweet girl. My struggles are coming to a close. My final goal is in sight. Soon, I will emerge in complete beauty and fly away with my precious Lord.

What a blessing you have been to me in my final years. What a precious gift God gave to me when He sent me you!

I am ending this letter with a fervent prayer for you. I know that after all these years of praying with me, you would expect it.

Our, dear heavenly Father, I thank you for this godly young woman. I pray that blessings will be showered down on my sweet Lily.

Give her courage, strength, and wisdom. But most of all, Lord, give her a loving heart. Help her to remember that without love, she is a sounding gong. Continue to guide Lily on the path that she should follow. I know, Lord, that you have wonderful things in store for her. Wonderful plans. Thank you for your loving kindness. In Jesus's name, amen.

Love,
Evelyn

Evelyn flew away with her Lord and Savior on the last day of spring.

I met Momma and Daisy at the funeral. It was a lovely celebration of her life. Most of her dear old friends were there. We talked and remembered Evelyn with tears and laughter. Afterwards, I drove to our house. It was strange walking up the steps and looking over, knowing that Evelyn wasn't next door anymore.

When I walked inside, I was surprised to see Mildred sitting in Roy's favorite chair. Daisy told me that Evelyn brought her over when she had to go to the hospital. She asked Daisy if she could watch her while she was gone. I reached down and gave old Mildred a pat. She purred and gave me her usual greeting of little short meows.

When I walked into my bedroom, there was a box on my bed. Momma told me that Evelyn had brought it over for me a few weeks back. I pulled off the tape and opened the lid. Inside the box was the entire set of her china with the hand-painted violets. There were also several packs of perennial seeds from her garden and her strand of pearls. Evelyn had enclosed a note. It said:

> Lily,
>
> May these three keepsakes always be a reminder of my love for you. Each one has its own lesson to remember in your daily walk with the Lord. They are as follows:
> When you use your china, I want you to look at it and remember to always keep your cup turned up so you may receive God's blessings. (Ps. 23:1–4)
> Next, as you plant these seeds and watch as God's beauty springs forth from the ground, also remember to plant seeds for God's kingdom wherever you go. (2 Cor. 9:6)
> Finally, when you wear your pearls, always remember that your real treasure is in heaven. (Matt. 13:44–45)
>
> Love,
> Evelyn

Daisy came and stood in my doorway. I showed her everything in the box and let her read Evelyn's letter. Daisy cried and said that she was really going to miss Evelyn. I told her that I was too.

I asked Daisy how Roy liked having Mildred around. She said he didn't mind her too much. She said that Mildred made quite a fuss when Roy came home wanting to sit in his lap and purring. She said that Momma thinks he likes the extra attention. Daisy said that she didn't have the heart to tell him that Mildred was making a fuss because he was sitting in her new chair!

Daisy went to her room and came back with a beautiful glass figurine of a girl holding a bouquet of flowers. She told me that Evelyn had brought it when she brought the box over for me. I teased her about the time she picked Evelyn's flowers and gave them to her. We laughed remembering that day.

Evelyn also gave Daisy the recipe for her famous oatmeal raisin cookies. Momma said that Evelyn gave her a book on growing plants and flowers. She said that she was excited to try some new techniques this summer.

Evelyn always knew what everyone needed. Her kindness and thoughtfulness never ceased to amaze me. My heart still aches a little when I think of her. Then I remember that I'll get to see her again someday in our eternal heavenly home.

CHAPTER 24

Finding Your Road Signs

Evelyn had such a great influence on me during our years as neighbors. I know that God himself must have reached down and guided Evelyn as she loved and taught me. None of this would have happened if Evelyn had not been blessed with a true servant's heart. She listened to her heavenly Father and she obeyed. As she lived out her time here on earth, she went about her days storing up riches in heaven, which glorified the Father and, in turn, blessed her beyond measure.

As followers of Jesus, we all are expected to listen to the Holy Spirit as He guides us. We all have a responsibility to love others and point them to Jesus just like Evelyn did.

Throughout my adult life, I have often thought about the many recipes for the heart that Evelyn shared with me. The scriptures and stories are always in the back of my mind when different circumstances arise. Just the other day, I was driving down a little two-lane county highway. I was tired and stressed from life's circumstances. As I drove along, I spotted a small handmade wooden sign. It had two words painted on it that said, "KEEP GOING."

As I drove past the sign, I couldn't help but smile to myself. I thought about how Evelyn would have a recipe for that sign. She would have said, "Lily, you see that sign over there? That is what God says to us every day. He wants you to keep going. He doesn't want you to give up and quit. He wants to make you strong in your weakness. He wants to give you courage and endurance. He wants you to run your race all the way to the end. He wants you to experience victory through Him."

Different Bible verses started to come to my mind as I thought about the two simple words, "KEEP GOING." This scripture is one that sticks with me:

> Do you not know that in a race all the runners run, but only one gets the prize? Run in such a way as to get the prize. Everyone who competes in the games goes into strict training. They do it to get a crown that will not last,

but we do it to get a crown that will last FOREVER. (1 Cor. 9:24–26)

Another verse that I come back to is:

Let us not become weary in doing good, for at the proper time we will reap a harvest if we do not give up. (Gal. 6:9)

The last verse that I hold dear is:

He gives strength to the weary and increases the power of the weak. Even youths grow tired and weary, and young men stumble and fall; but those who hope in the Lord will renew their strength. They will soar on wings like eagles; they will run and not grow weary, they will walk and not be faint. (Isa. 40:29–31)

Like the saints before me, I, too, keep going. I wake up each day and decide to live a life that is pleasing to God. I still fail from time to time. I say and do things sometimes and have to ask God and others to forgive me. But I keep running this race. I realize that only with God's help, I can find the endurance that I need.

Although my life is full of ups and downs, I still try to notice if there is anyone who may need a recipe for the heart. When I find that someone, I always attempt to share. I'm often reminded of Evelyn's favorite saying. She would always tell me that "a recipe for the heart can be such a blessing when it comes from the Lord's recipe box."

So like my friend Evelyn, I, too, try to be a good and faithful servant and share the Lord's recipes for the heart.

GOD'S RECIPES
TO REMEMBER

God's Love

Give thanks to the God of heaven,
for His steadfast love endures forever.
(Ps. 136:26)

But you, Lord are a compassionate
and gracious God, slow to anger,
abounding in love and faithfulness.
(Ps. 86:15)

I have loved you with an everlasting
love; I have drawn you with unfailing
kindness. (Jer. 31:3)

This is how God showed His love
among us: He sent His one and only
Son into the world that we might live
through Him. This is love: not that
we loved God, but that He loved us
and sent His Son as an atoning sacrifice for our sins. (1 John 4:9–10)

God's Plan for Mankind

> God created man in His own Image,
> in the image of God He created him;
> male and female, He created them.
> (Gen. 1:27)

> When I consider your heavens, the
> work of your fingers, the moon and
> the stars, which you have set in place,
> what is mankind that you are mind-
> ful of them, human beings that you
> care for them? You have made them
> a little lower than the angels and
> crowned them with glory and honor.
> (Ps. 8:3–5)

God's Faithfulness

> If we confess our sins, He is faithful
> and just and will forgive us our sins
> and purify us from all unrighteous-
> ness. (1 John 1:9)

> If we are faithless, He remains faith-
> ful, for He cannot deny Himself.
> (2 Tim. 2:13)

> The Lord is faithful, who will estab-
> lish you and guard you from the evil
> one. (2 Thess. 3:3)

Your faithfulness endures to all gen-
erations; you have established the
earth, and it stands fast. (Ps. 119:90)

Because of the Lord's great love we
are not consumed. For His compas-
sions never fail. They are new every
morning; Great is Your faithfulness.
(Lam. 3:22–23)

God's Trinity

Now it is God who makes both us
and you stand firm in Christ. He
anointed us, set His seal of ownership
on us, and put His Spirit in our hearts
as a deposit, guaranteeing what is to
come. (2 Cor. 1:21–22)

According to the foreknowledge of
God the Father, by the sanctifying
work of the Spirit, to obey Jesus
Christ and be sprinkled with His
blood: may grace and peace be yours
in the fullest measure. (1 Pet. 1:2)

A cord of three strands is not quickly
broken. (Eccles. 4:12b)

May the grace of the Lord Jesus
Christ, and the love of God, and the

fellowship of the Holy Spirit be with you all. (2 Cor. 3:17)

Being Kind

Therefore, as God's chosen people, holy and dearly loved, clothe yourselves with compassion, kindness, humility, gentleness and patience. (Col. 3:12)

Be merciful to those who doubt; save others by snatching them from the fire; to others show mercy, mixed with fear—hating even the clothing stained by corrupted flesh. (Jude 1:22–23)

Gracious words are a honeycomb, sweet to the soul and healing to the bones. (Prov. 16:24)

Do not forget to show hospitality to strangers, for by doing so, some people have shown hospitality to angels without knowing it. (Heb. 13:2)

Humility

Humble yourselves before the Lord, and He will lift you up. (James 4:10)

For all those who exalt themselves will be humbled, and those who humble themselves will be exalted. (Luke 14:11)

For by the grace given me I say to every one of you: Do not think yourself more highly than you ought, but rather think of yourself with sober judgement, in accordance with the faith God has distributed to each of you. (Rom. 12:3)

Humility is the fear of the Lord; its wages are riches and honor and life. (Prov. 22:4)

Courage

What then shall we say to these things? If God is for us, who is against us? (Rom. 8:31)

Put on the full armor of God, so that you can take your stand against the devil's schemes. (Eph. 6:11)

Take the helmet of salvation and the sword of the Spirit, which is the word of God. (Eph. 6:17)

Have I not commanded you? Be strong and courageous. Do not be afraid; do not be discouraged, for the Lord your God will be with you wherever you go. (Josh. 1:9)

Strength

Let us acknowledge the Lord; let us press on to acknowledge Him. As surely as the sun rises, He will appear; He will come to us like the winter rains, like the spring rains that water the earth. (Hosea 6:3)

But you are a chosen people, a royal priesthood, a holy nation, God's special possession, that you may declare the praises of Him who called you out of darkness into His wonderful light. (1 Pet. 2:9)

I will refresh the weary and satisfy the faint. (Jer. 31:25)

Endurance

Consider it pure joy, my brothers and sisters, whenever you face trials of many kinds, because you know that the testing of your faith produces perseverance. (James. 1:2–3)

Be joyful in hope, patient in affliction, faithful in prayer. (Rom. 12:12)

May the God who gives endurance and encouragement give you the same attitude of mind toward each other that Christ had. (Rom. 15:5)

I can do all this through Him who gives me strength. (Phil. 4:13)

Walking on Holy Ground

And pray in the Spirit on all occasions with all kinds of prayers and requests. With this in mind, be alert and always keep on praying for all the Lord's people. (Eph. 6:18)

Then you will call on me and come and pray to me, and I will listen to you. (Jer. 29:12)

Worship the Lord in the splendor of His holiness; tremble before Him, all the earth. (Ps. 96:9)

"Holy, holy, holy is the Lord God Almighty, who was, and is, and is to come." (Rev. 4:8b)

"Take off your sandals, for the place where you are standing is holy ground." (Exod. 3:5)

Usefulness

Now you are the body of Christ, and each one of you is a part of it. (1 Cor. 12:27)

For just as we have many members in one body and all the members do not have the same function, so we, who are many, are one body in Christ, and individually members one of another. (Rom. 12:4–5)

We have different gifts, according to the grace given to each of us. If your gift is prophesying, then prophesy in accordance with your faith, if it is serving, then serve; if it is teaching, then teach; if it is to encourage, then give encouragement; if it is giving, then give generously; if it is to lead, do it diligently; if it is to show mercy, do it cheerfully. (Rom. 12:6–8)

Prayer

"This, then, is how you should pray: 'Our Father in heaven, hallowed be your name, your kingdom come, your will be done, on earth as it is in heaven. Give us today our daily bread. And forgive us our debts, as we also have forgiven our debtors. And lead us not into temptation, but deliver us from the evil one.'" (Matt. 6:9–13)

"Again, truly I tell you that if two of you on earth agree about anything they ask for, it will be done for them by my Father in heaven. For where two or three gather in my name, there am I with them." (Matt. 18:18–19)

When you pray, go to your room and close the door. Pray privately to your Father who is with you. Your Father will see what you do in private. He will reward you. (Matt. 6:6–8)

In the same way the Spirit also helps our weakness; for we do not know how to pray as we should, but the Spirit Himself intercedes for us with groanings too deep for words; and He who searches the heart knows what the mind of the Spirit is, because He intercedes for the saints according to the will of God. (Rom. 8:26–27)

Forgiveness

For if you forgive other people when they sin against you, your heavenly Father will also forgive you. But if you do not forgive others their sins, your Father will not forgive your sins. (Matt. 6:14–15)

Repent, then, and turn to God, so that your sins may be wiped out, that times of refreshing may come from the Lord. (Acts 3:19)

Get rid of all bitterness, rage and anger, brawling and slander, along with every form of malice. Be kind and compassionate to one another, forgiving each other, just as in Christ God forgave you. (Eph. 4:31–32)

Faith

Trust in the Lord with all your heart and lean not on your own under-standing; in all your ways submit to

him, and he will make your paths
straight. (Prov. 3:5–6)

The righteous cry out, and the Lord
hears them; he delivers them from all
their troubles. The Lord is close to the
brokenhearted and saves those who
are crushed in spirit. (Ps. 34:17–18)

Dear friends, do not be surprised
at the fiery ordeal that has come on
you to test you, as though something
strange were happening to you. But
rejoice inasmuch as you participate
in the sufferings of Christ, so that
you may be overjoyed when his glory
is revealed. (1 Pet. 4:12–14)

Hope

For I know the plans I have for you,
declares the Lord, plans to prosper
you and not to harm you, plans to give
you hope and a future. (Jer. 29:11)

Praise be to the God and Father of our
Lord Jesus Christ! In his great mercy
he has given us new birth into a living hope through the resurrection of
Jesus Christ from the dead, and into

an inheritance that can never perish,
spoil or fade. (1 Pet. 1:3–4)

May the God of hope fill you with
all joy and peace as you trust in him,
so that you may overflow with hope
by the power of the Holy Spirit.
(Rom. 15:13)

Salvation

That if you confess with your mouth,
"Jesus is Lord," and believe in your
heart that God raised him from the
dead, you will be saved. For it is with
your heart that you believe and are
justified, and it is with your mouth
that you confess and are saved.
(Rom. 10:9–10)

God made him who had no sin to be
sin for us, so that in him we might
become the righteousness of God.
(2 Cor. 5:21)

For it is by grace you have been saved,
through faith-and this is not from
yourselves, it is the gift of God-not
by works, so that no one can boast.
(Eph. 2:8–9)